LOST

IN THE DEEP WOODS

LOST

IN THE DEEP WOODS

A NOVEL

DAWN BATTERBEE MILLER

DocUmeant Publishing
244 5th Avenue, Suite G200
NY, NY 10001
Phone: 6462334366

http://www.DocUmeantPublishing.com

ISBN 13: 9781937801427
ISBN 10: 193780142X
Library of Congress Catalog Card Number: 2012909541

I want to express my thanks to all those friends and acquaintances, who have waited impatiently for the sequel to *Footprints Under the Pines,* and spurred me on to completion.

FOREWORD

FOOTPRINTS UNDER THE Pines, the first book in the Deep Woods series, relates the events of the McLean family as they make their way from Ontario, Canada to the lumber camps of Northern Michigan. We watch as the family sets out across Lake Huron in a rowboat and settles in the little town of Hitchcock—deep woods lumbering territory.

Eventually the family enters the lumber camp culture and a totally new life experience begins. They live in the deep woods and participate in the harvest of the giant pines that are said to be big enough to build a house with only one tree.

But an empty hole exists in Hannah McLean's heart. She lost her mother to consumption when she was a baby, her father, Frank McLean, to the deep woods and her brother when the family moved from Canada.

Lost in the Deep Woods picks up the saga as Hannah runs through the forest, to find her long lost brother.

CHAPTER 1

TURMOIL CHURNED IN Hannah McLean's bones as she raced along Birch Lake Road. Blue jays chattered in the trees, and sweat bees swirled around her head. She swatted at the bees, trying to clear her mind of the muddle that shrouded her senses. In her hand, she clutched a note.

> *Dear Hannah,*
> *I'm on my way to Hitchcock. Should be there around noon on Monday. Meet me by the tracks. And please don't tell anyone I'm coming.*
> *Seth*

As the young woman came near the tracks, she stopped. There was nothing in sight but the immense pine trees that overspread the land in every direction. Only the iron railway disrupted the woodland, streaming its way into oblivion in either direction.

"Hannah?"

Hannah turned to see her brother, taller and thinner than she remembered, with a veil of darkness shadowing his face. "Seth, what's the matter? What happened?"

Seth peered at Hannah with passionate resolve. "Sis," he said. "I need a place to stay for a few days."

"Great. Come home with me," Hannah responded. "Everyone will be excited to see you."

"No, I can't come to the house. What I need is a place to stay . . . without a lot of people around."

"Why? What's wrong?"

"I can't talk about it. Please, sis, just find me a place to stay."

Confusion ensnarled Hannah's thinking. What could have happened to prevent Seth from coming home with her? She reached out and touched her brother's arm. Whatever the problem, she would not lose him again. She swallowed the tension that had risen in her throat and then performed a mental search of the area. There was the cave on the backside of Parson's Dome—no, it was likely that her neighbors would be wandering around back there. She thought about the sugaring-off building beside Bear Lake, but the place was swarming with wasps. She thought about the overhang that sheltered the dry riverbed at Swartz Pass—no, it was far too open to passersby.

"I know," she said at last. "There's a shack in the gully at Little Birch Lake. No one ever goes there because the slope is so steep you have to pull yourself up the hill by grabbing onto the trees. You could stay there forever and no one would know."

"That sounds perfect; let's go."

Hannah led the way toward the gorge. It wouldn't be as good as having Seth at home, but it was a lot better than Ontario.

Soon Hannah and Seth found themselves looking into a deep chasm. The ground was studded with oaks and maples and poplars. It sloped downward so quickly that it almost made Hannah's head spin.

"This is unbelievable," Seth said, as he descended the grade. "It's no wonder . . . no one ever . . . comes here. It's just the . . . right place . . . for me." He reached for another branch, clinging to it for support.

At the bottom of the gully, Hannah and Seth found an old abandoned shack whose hasp had long since been torn loose.

The door sagged on its hinges until it dragged on the ground and had long ago traced an arc in the dirt where it swung. They entered through the sagging portal.

Inside, the siblings found total disorder with trash piled everywhere. In one corner lay a torn and tattered old bed-tick with spikes of straw sticking through its rotting fabric. A little heater stood nearby, vented through a smokestack in the back wall. On top of the stove sat an old cooking pot. The only other furnishings were a three-legged stool and a table, cobbled together out of two sawhorses with boards laid across them.

"Well, it isn't much," Hannah said. "Are you sure you want to stay here? You could still come home with me, you know."

Seth was adamant. "I'm sure; this'll be fine. I'll clear out the trash and it won't be so bad."

"Well, if you won't change your mind . . ."

"I can't, Hannah. I need time to think."

Hannah's heart fell. "Well then, we better get to cleaning." Something bordering on fear settled in her gut as she reached for a broom.

"No," Seth said, "I'll clean after you leave. Right now I just want to visit." He laid his bag on the straw tick and found a perch on the makeshift table. "What's going on with you and the family?"

"Nothing much," Hannah responded. She seated herself on the stool. "Mostly, I've been excited about the fact that you were coming."

"Me, too. It's good to see you."

"Do you remember the day we went fishing in Strom's Creek and you slipped trying to catch a frog? You got soaked up to your waist."

"Or the jar of peaches we took from the cellar and went out into the garden to eat?"

"And Grandma found the jar. She washed it and left in on the kitchen table for days and never said a word."

"We felt guilty every time we looked at it."

The two siblings talked of life and living and old times. They laughed and joked and conversed.

"Well, Seth," Hannah said as the hour grew late, "I guess I better go back home before they miss me."

A melancholy air swept over Seth's face. "Hannah," he said, "I haven't felt this good for a long time."

"It's been great to be here with you," Hannah responded. "You can't possibly know how I've missed you. Won't you please come home with me?"

"No," Seth said. "I . . ." He turned his face away, brushing his hand over his eyes, "I gotta stay here where I can think."

With that, Hannah took her leave, promising to return with supplies as soon as she could.

Seth watched as his sister made her way up the slope under the budding canopy. She reached for a sapling, pulled herself upward, and disappeared among the trees. He'd asked her to do an unthinkable task. He'd asked her to harbor a fugitive.

Turning, he surveyed his surroundings. Leeks and trillium and adder's-tongue dotted the ground. He could see a blackberry patch off to his left, green and without fruit. He bent and gathered a handful of beechnuts from the tree that arched over his new shanty home. He cracked open the tiny morsels and popped them into his mouth.

Then he looked out at the nearby lake. He took in a narrow spit that extended from the shore with a sweep of watercress along its edge. If he were desperate, he might gather some of those leaves for a meal—not really great, but edible if needed, and they'd help to fill his stomach.

I wonder if there are fish in that lake, he thought. Later he'd rig up a line and try it out, but just now he needed a break. The young man breathed a sigh, entered the shanty, and lay on the tattered old tick. It sagged under his weight and was hardly a comfortable bed, but he soon fell asleep.

Chapter 2

IT WAS NEAR midnight, and the moon shone brightly through the window of Hannah's new home at Camp 8. Hannah's family had purchased the cutover lumber camp several years ago and moved into the cook shanty. The lumberjacks who had lived here many years ago had taken their meals in this building.

Hannah lay staring into the night, waiting for time to pass.

Faith Ann slept soundly on the bed beside her, breathing in a slow, even rhythm. Katherine and Clive had retired to their room several hours earlier. It was time for Hannah to make her move.

Silently she crawled from beneath the sheets and slipped into her clothing. She reached for several jars of canned goods and a loaf of bread she had stored on the shelf above her head. Then she grabbed an old cooking pot she'd found deep in the cupboard, put the bread inside and wrapped the supplies in a blanket. Finally, she reached into her pocket, fingering a handful of matches, a jackknife, and a fishhook with some line.

Slowly the young woman took her jacket from a nail by the entry, pulled it around her shoulders, and reached for the package. She stepped outside into a bright moonlit night and closed the door ever so softly. A tiny click announced that it was latched. She turned and as she did, Wolf growled and rose from his old quilt bed on the porch. "Shhhh," Hannah whispered. "It's only me." She patted the family dog's side, and he grew quiet. Then she put the bundle she'd packed in Faith Ann's wagon and reached for the handle. "C'mon, Wolf," she murmured. "You can keep me company."

Nearing the chasm where her brother waited, Hannah stopped and looked around. What if she were caught? Would her brother be wrenched from her again? Seth was the only family she had now that her pa was gone, and she'd do just about anything to keep him safe—safe from what? What horrible news was her brother hiding?

Arriving at the gorge, she dragged the wagon off the road, lifted the package into her arms, and started down the incline. Wolf came along, yipping and complaining all the way. Then, as they came near the bottom of the gorge, the dog barked.

"Hush," Hannah snapped. "You'll wake the whole world." It was only a moment's inattention, but it was too late. Her feet slid from beneath her on the slippery turf, and the supplies flew into the air, scattering all across the duff. "Ughhh!" She slammed into a tree and Wolf came chasing after her, hovering about like a knight in shining armor.

"It's okay, Wolf," she gasped. "I'm fine." She pushed the dog aside and rose to her feet, looking around for the lost provisions. Just then something moved in the darkness and Wolf growled.

He stood alert—stiff and unyielding, trembling in agitation. Hannah peered intently into the brush but saw nothing.

Finally a voice wafted on the air, soft and quiet. "Hannah, is that you?"

Hannah sighed with relief. "Yes, Seth, it's me. I'm over here." Hannah's brother moved closer and Wolf's hackles stood on end. "It's okay, Wolf," Hannah said. "He's my brother."

The dog remained tense, ready to lunge. Hannah brushed her hand over Wolf's shoulders, patting his side and rubbing his flank. "Calm down," she commanded. "He's a friend."

Finally, Seth appeared out of the darkness. He came near and waited while Wolf sniffed at his clothing, smelled his fingertips, and gave up the fight.

"Good dog," Hannah said.

At that point the two young people gathered what they could find of Hannah's provisions and headed downward into the gulch. They entered the hut, lit only by the bright moonlight that shone through the window and through the open door.

Hannah laid the provisions on the makeshift table, and Seth tossed the bedding on the tattered old tick. Scanning the supplies, the young man reached for a jar of stew. "Did you happen to bring a spoon?" he said.

Hannah's jaw dropped. "No, I didn't even think of it."

Seth tipped the container to his lips and consumed its contents without need for amenities. "Mmmmmm, that was good," he mumbled.

"Well, it'll do for now, anyway." Hannah pulled the jackknife from her pocket, along with the matches and fishing gear. "I thought you might be able to use these," she said. She put the supplies on the table and seated herself on the stool.

"Perfect," Seth responded. "I was thinking there ought to be fish in that lake and now, with this stuff, I can go after them."

Hannah's heart swelled. "Next thing you know you'll be dining on crappies and rainbow trout." She moved toward the door. "I better go now before Faith Ann wakes up. She's sleeping in my bed, and if she wakes up and misses me it won't be good."

"I suppose," Seth responded, "but come back when you can. I'll be waiting."

Hannah stepped through the sagging portal and into the night. "Are you sure you won't come with me?"

"Not today . . . and not soon."

The siblings stood facing each other for several long moments, each filled with his or her inward emotions. Then Seth stepped back. "You're a lifesaver," he whispered.

7

"I'll be back tomorrow with whatever I can find," Hannah said.

Then she led Wolf up the hill toward home.

Twenty minutes later Hannah and Wolf arrived at the cook shanty. Wolf found his bed on the porch, and Hannah slipped inside, tiptoeing toward the space behind the wall where her sister lay sleeping. As she entered Faith Ann sat upright, rubbing her eyes with her fingers. "Hannah, where you been?"

"Ah. . . um. . . I just..." The young woman's heart beat a tattoo in her chest. "I went outside to the toilet."

"Well you sure was gone a long time."

"Maybe, but I'm here now and everything's okay, so you can go back to sleep." Hannah crawled into bed beside the girl and wrapped herself around her for warmth. Faith Ann snuggled close and soon her breathing slackened. Hannah's sister returned to dreamland.

But Hannah lay awake, pondering Seth's arrival. How did he get here? Why was he so secretive? Should she demand an explanation? What if she did? Would it make him mad? Maybe he was involved in some crime—and so what if he was? She'd never turn him in. She wasn't about to give up her brother now that she'd found him.

CHAPTER 3

KATHERINE ISAMAN STOOD with her husband, Clive, viewing the cutover logging camp that had become their home. "Clive, I'm worried about Hannah," she said.

Clive gazed across the fields with his mind in another world. "Do you see what I see?" he responded. "I see crops of corn and oats and wheat that will one day grow on this, our land."

"But what about Hannah?" Katherine's concern about her stepdaughter wouldn't be assuaged.

"Why, what has she done?"

"It's not what she's done; it's what she hasn't done." Katherine flicked a hair out of her face. "She doesn't communicate anymore. She's disconnected. I don't think she's accepted her life out here."

"Well, don't worry." Clive slipped his arm around his wife's shoulder. "The girl just needs a little time."

Katherine sighed and continued her explanation. "She leaves the house without telling me where she's going. Then when she comes in, she mumbles something about having lost track of time."

"Well, let's just wait and see," Clive said. "These things happen with young people. She'll be okay. Don't worry about it."

"I do worry," Katherine said. "She goes off for long periods of time and then doesn't want to talk about it. I can't help it; I worry."

Suddenly Faith Ann came running around the barn. "Mama," she yelled. "Mr. Clive, there's a sick dog out there and he's stumbling all over the place. He's rubbing his nose on the ground and spitting on everything." The little girl stopped short, gasping for breath. Then she grabbed her mother's hand, heading toward the barn.

Katherine followed her daughter, and Clive came close behind. As they rounded the corner a red fox came into view, staggering and stumbling along the fence line. He lurched and fell. Then he rose to his feet and fell again. A strand of mucus slavered from his mouth, leaving a trail of dribble in its wake.

"It's a fox," Clive shouted. "And he's rabid. Where's my gun?" He turned and ran toward the cook shanty, returning shortly with his weapon.

"Mama, what's rabid?" Faith Ann said.

"Well, a rabid animal is one that's really, really sick—so sick he's going to die very soon."

"But if the fox is sick, he needs our help. Mr. Clive shouldn't shoot him."

Katherine reached out to the girl. "Sweetheart," she said, "an animal with rabies is going to die. He can't ever get over it, and everyone and everything that comes in contact with him will get the rabies."

Faith Ann's brow furrowed. "And then I guess they'll all die too," she said. "But the fox shouldn't be shot just because he's sick."

"Well, that's the only way we know to deal with him."

A grimace flashed across Faith Ann's face. "I remember when my pa died," she said. "I still get lonesome for him sometimes."

"I know, sweetheart. I miss him too, but he's gone now. Mr. Clive is your pa, and he loves you very much." Katherine's mind flashed back to her first husband, Frank McLean, who had married her even though she carried another man's child. She thought about Clive, who had gone off to the lumber camps without knowing she had conceived. And she thought about Frank's death and her marriage to Clive, Faith Ann's father. Clive never knew he'd fathered a child until Frank lost his life in the woods and he sought to marry Katherine.

Katherine brushed her hand over her abdomen. How long should she wait before she told Clive about this new life he'd created? She smiled inwardly, knowing it would please him to be present when this child came into the world.

Clive stalked across the field with his eyes trained on the tree line. He moved slowly and deliberately, watching for any sign of the rabid fox. He walked and watched and listened, but all was silent and still. At one point, he thought he caught a glimpse of the animal, but the creature disappeared into the brush and he failed to get a shot. Tomorrow he'd set traps.

Finally he turned and walked toward Camp 8 and as he did a rabbit burst from the scrub and skittered across the ground, bounding toward a brush pile. Clive lifted his weapon, sighted down the barrel, and pulled the trigger. His prey lay immobile. He tucked his gun under one arm, picked up the fallen buck and made his way home with his prize. There'd be fresh meat for supper tonight—a good piece of work for a wilderness farmer.

The next morning, after Clive set traps for the fox, he made his way to the men's shanty, a typical lumber-camp shelter with bunks along the walls. A clothesline had been stretched across the room, and a heater stood in the center with a spit-box by its side. Clive had big plans for this building. After he had furnished it with a workbench, shelves, and tools, it would become his space. It would contain everything a man might need to run a farm, but today he needed to get those seed potatoes cut and ready for planting.

Turning, he reached for a six-inch board, planning to make a splitter. He laid the board across a shelf, embedded a sharp knife into it, and placed the device across two sawhorses. Then he climbed astride the apparatus with the knife pointing upward between his knees. He selected a potato from a crate on his right. He looked at it for sprouts, slid the tuber over the cutting edge and swiped again.

He had created three cuttings, each with a bud that would germinate and grow. Then he tossed the seedlings into the bag on his left.

At that moment the door burst open and Faith Ann came hurtling through. "Mr. Clive, Mr. Clive." She threw herself at her father, leaning over his knee with her face in his line of vision and her back far too close to the knife.

In an instant, Clive grabbed his daughter's arm and yanked her away from the device. "Be careful," he said. "That blade is sharp enough to cut out your gizzard."

Faith Ann stepped back, frowning. "What's a gizzard?" she said. "Do I have a gizzard?"

"Well, no." Clive grinned at his daughter. "A gizzard is something that helps chickens to digest their food. That was just my way of telling you to be careful or you'd get hurt."

For a moment Faith Ann stood contemplating the matter. Then she stepped back and voiced the complaint that had brought her to the building in the first place. "Mr. Clive," she said, "Hannah won't let me go to the spring with her. She says she doesn't want to wait for me, but I'm all ready, and she still won't take me along."

"Well, don't get upset." Clive pointed toward the crate by his side. "You just stay here with me and we'll get these potatoes ready to plant."

Faith Ann's face drew into a pout. "But I want to go with Hannah."

Clive stopped and pulled his daughter close. "Sometimes big girls just need to get away," he said. "And I think that's probably what Hannah needs today."

"Well, what do you want me to do?"

"Just hand me those seedlings one at a time," Clive responded, "and I'll cut them into buds. Together we'll get enough to sow a whole field tomorrow."

Faith Ann reached into the gunnysack, drew out a potato, and handed it to her father.

"Come fall, we'll sell the crop and buy you a new dress before school starts."

Pure delight spread crossed Faith Ann's face. "A new dress!" she said. The girl reached for another potato. "I'll buy the prettiest dress in the whole Sears catalogue."

Clive grinned as his little girl became involved and forgot about Hannah. He set his mind on the job at hand.

Tomorrow he'd drag chains over the south twenty to mark rows and then walk the field. He'd drop the seedlings into a planter, plunge the device into the ground, and step forward. As he walked, the jaws would open and drop the seedling into the moist earth. In time the plants would germinate and grow, and he'd have a fine crop of potatoes to harvest.

Seth walked along the forest's edge, collecting rocks and carrying them back to the shack at Birch Lake gorge. Near the building, he arranged the stones in a circle around a pile of kindling. It was hard work, but when he was finished, he'd have a fire pit to cook his meals.

As he laid the last rock in place, he stepped back, taking stock of the project. It was okay—no, downright good. Later he'd repair the old shack and plant a garden. In time, the place might become quite pleasant.

At that point the young man retrieved the fishing gear Hannah had brought and headed for the lake. He found a likely fishing spot, tossed the line into the water, and sat on the bank, letting his mind wander back to the farm in Ontario. He thought about Grandma and Grandpa McLean, and his heart ached. He knew they must have been confused and lost and hurt when he left. It had been his intention to stay with them and carry on the work when they could no longer manage the place, but it could never be. He could never go back.

Suddenly the rod jerked and Seth's attention was focused on the moment. He drew the line tight, waited until the tension eased, and pulled again. He pulled and waited and pulled and waited, drawing the fish ever nearer the shore, until at last his trophy flopped at his feet. He reached out, grabbed it by the gills, and removed the hook. Finally he headed back to the shack.

There he built a fire, filleted his prize, and waited as the aroma of fresh-roasted crappie wafted on the air. At last he gathered some of Hannah's bread, dipped a jar of the crystal clear drinking water from the lake, and consumed the repast. It was the best meal he'd had in some time.

CHAPTER 4

MAY THE LORD go with you and bring you safely to His house again next week." Parson Tibbs said the benediction, moved toward the back of the church, and dismissed the congregation.

Hannah rose and walked with her family toward the exit, glad for their departure. Although she enjoyed the singing and visiting with friends, she felt the parson's sermons were far too long, and he had a way of harping on things that were none of his business. "Have a good week," the parson said as Uncle Ned stepped near the door.

"Thank you, Pastor," Uncle Ned responded. "And you do the same." Clive reached out to Parson Tibbs in a hearty handshake. "Good sermon this morning, Pastor," he said.

Hannah's lips curled in disagreement. *Secret sins indeed! It wasn't any of that preacher's business if she had a secret.* She slipped past the reverend as quickly as possible. Outside, she noticed a stranger, lean of stature with sandy hair that was straight and combed to one side. He stood silent and remote in his blue pants and shirt, observing each individual as he or she passed by. His demeanor left Hannah with a sense of unease. She wasn't sure why. Turning, she walked directly to the family carriage, climbed in, and settled herself.

It wasn't long before Faith Ann came running toward the buggy. Then Clive and Katherine ambled easily along, making their way in their own time. Finally, when everyone was aboard the transport, Clive flicked the reins. "Giddap," he called, and the carriage traveled westward along Hitchcock Road and around Parson's Dome. Uncle Ned's place and Sunday dinner were just beyond the peak.

Soon the buggy came to a stop near the house, and Hannah climbed onto the ground with Faith Ann and Katherine. Clive unhitched the horses and put them out to graze.

As the ladies stepped into the cabin, Aunt Mae began giving instructions. "Hannah, you get a leaf out of the closet," she said, "and Katherine'll help you put it in place. Then you and Faith Ann can set the table, while Katherine and I get the meal started."

Hannah's lips curved into a half smile. Wasn't that just like Aunt Mae? The woman was as goodhearted as they come, but she simply had to have everything in her command. Nevertheless, Hannah had to admit that when Aunt Mae was in charge, things ran smoothly. Hannah and Faith Ann began putting plates and silverware on the table.

In the kitchen Aunt Mae stirred the coals in the firepot and tossed in several small sticks, fanning the embers into flame. Everyone followed instructions, and soon the family dined on chicken and dumplings with mashed potatoes and corn and a good helping of summer squash. At last Aunt Mae served apple pie topped with whipped cream, a fine finish for a good Sunday meal.

As Uncle Ned downed the last of his dessert, he leaned back in his chair and sighed. "Well, Mae, you've done it again. The old man is as happy as a titmouse on an anthill."

"Thank you, Mae," Clive said. "Dinner was great, as usual."

Aunt Mae smiled and began clearing the table, while Katherine filled the dishpan with hot water from the teakettle and began washing dishes. Hannah and Faith Ann wiped the tableware as Aunt Mae put it away, stacking the plates, cups, and glasses in the cupboard in perfect order. She didn't want her dishes "strewn all over the place" by the girls.

"C'mon, Hannah," Faith Ann said as Hannah hung up her apron. "Let's go down to Brown Lake and see the ducks."

Hannah looked out the window at a beautiful spring afternoon. The sky was blue, the grass was green, and warm sunshine smiled down on all creation. "Sure; why not?" she said. She reached out to her little sister and they left the house, walking hand in hand down the lane. Soon they entered the woodland through a lush portal, where maple trees arched over the path in a verdant passageway.

Faith Ann ran about, exploring the undergrowth with its wildflowers and leeks and adder's-tongue. "Oh look, Hannah, flowers for Mama." The little girl bent to pick trilliums that grew along the path.

"Wait!" Hannah called. "Don't pick 'em yet. If we do it on our way back, they'll be fresh when we get home."

"Okay, but I want flowers for Mama and Aunt Mae."

17"That'll be nice, but let's get them later."

Faith Ann returned to Hannah's side and the girls walked together, listening to the birds twittering in the trees. There was nothing like an afternoon in the woodland on a warm spring day.

Soon the girls reached the clearing, and Brown Lake came into view. A gentle breeze wafted on the water, causing ripples that lapped onto the shore in a steady rhythm. Reeds poked their spines upward, and water lilies danced on the waves with dragonflies hovering over their leaves.

"Oh, look." Faith Ann pointed toward the south side of the lake, where two large black-and-white birds floated effortlessly on the water. "There they are! See 'em?"

"Sure enough, you found the ducks."

Faith Ann ran to the shore, tossing pebbles into its depths and watching the ever-widening ripples they created. "Look, Hannah," she called. "Look at the waves."

"Yes, I see," Hannah responded.

With that, the little girl dropped onto the sand and began building castles and digging moats where rivulets of water flowed past her creations.

Hannah found a place on the shore, basking in the warmth of the day and watching her little sister. She leaned back and let her mind wander through the past week with her brother . . . and before she knew it, her eyes grew heavy and she dozed.

Then in an instant, the young woman's reverie was shattered.

Two big ducks stood nipping at her toes.

Jumping to her feet, Hannah flung her arms at the birds. "Get out of here, you blithering idiots," she yelled. "Get out of here, and leave my feet alone."

Immediately the clamor of ruffled feathers and screeching fowl filled the air. Wings flapped and voices squawked. The atmosphere reverberated with the commotion.

Hannah scowled. "How dare you come ashore and bite my feet?" Then as the uproar died away, a penetrating silence invaded the environment. She looked around the beach. It was empty and void. Where was Faith Ann? "Faith Ann," Hannah called, "where are you?" The only sound was the ripple of the lake and a single crow calling out in the treetops. "Faith Ann, it's time to go."

There was no response, and Hannah stood breathless and paralyzed with fear. She remembered the time Faith Ann was kidnapped and the days and weeks the family searched for her. If Hannah lost the child now, she would kill herself. She turned, staring at the undulating water. Surely her sister wouldn't go into that cold lake. A sickening wave of terror welled up from the pit of Hannah's stomach. "O God, if there is a God, please help me find my little sister!"

The young woman moved away from the water's edge, making her way toward the deep grasses along the shore. "Faith Ann," she called again, "where are you?" Hannah shielded her eyes with her hand, peering across the reeds and seeing nothing. The fear in her abdomen intensified. Where was that girl? How dare she run away like this?

18

Suddenly the reeds broke, and Faith Ann came charging toward her sister. Hannah flung herself at the girl. "What do you think you're doing?"

"I'm sorry, Hannah." Faith Ann brushed her hand over her eyes. "I just got sleepy and laid down for a minute."

Hannah threw her arms around the girl and squeezed her into a bear hug. "Don't you ever disappear like that again!" she wailed. "You just about scared the wits out of me." She took Faith Ann's hand and headed back toward the shoreline. As she walked, she grinned within herself. After all, the child's nap was really no different than her own drowsiness.

Finally the girls headed home. They walked along, enjoying the tranquility of the forest. When they came near the place where the wildflowers grew, Faith Ann ran into the duff, darting from one plant to another, gathering the lilywhite trilliums for Katherine. "Flowers for Mama," she called. She shoved the bouquet into Hannah's hand and returned to the undergrowth. "Now I gotta get some for Aunt Mae."

They continued on their way, and finally the trees fell away and the girls broke from the woodland. "Mama," Faith Ann yelled. She reached for the flowers and ran ahead. "Mama, I got lilies for you." Hannah meandered along, enjoying the day.

Soon Hannah came within earshot of the barn and noticed voices wafting on the air. "The guy comes from Canada," Uncle Ned said. "He just stood there by himself, eyeing everyone as they walked by. He didn't seem to have any connection with anyone or anything."

"Yes," Clive responded. "I noticed. He just hung around the church doors, as if he were watching for someone or something."

Hannah froze in her tracks. Seth hadn't wanted anyone to know he was here—he didn't want to be found. Was that man looking for Seth? Hannah's shoulders stiffened into a block of ice. Well, so what if he was? Hannah wasn't about to lose her brother again to some stupid intruder. She set her jaw and stalked away.

The remainder of the day was filled with talk and laughter and jokes. Then late in the afternoon, the Isamans climbed into their buggy and took their leave, returning to their new lumber-camp home.

It was Monday morning, and Clive busied himself cleaning and updating the men's shanty. He pulled down the clothesline and tossed it into a trash box. He could only imagine the stench that had filled this place as a horde of dirty, sweaty socks hung on that line to dry. He picked up a board that lay in the middle of the room and leaned it against a wall. Maybe one day he'd use that piece of timber to build a workbench for his new tool shed.

Nearby, Faith Ann wandered around the room, poking at things and examining the furnishings. "Hey, Mr. Clive," she called. "How come they got a sandbox in here?"

"Ugh," Clive yelled. "Don't touch that thing. It's filthy."

"I wasn't going to touch it," Faith Ann responded, "but why would they put a sandbox in the house? Wouldn't it be better to put it outdoors, where it wouldn't get dirt all over the floor?"

"Actually, that isn't a sandbox," Clive said. "It's a spit-box. This used to be home to a bunch of big, tough lumbermen who worked hard all day, and when they came back here, they stood around and chewed tobacco and told stories." Clive brushed his hand across his overalls, as if to wipe off the dirt. "Then when their mouth got full of tobacco juice, they spit it into that box."

"Ugh," Faith Ann said. "That sounds awful. We better throw that thing away."

Clive grinned and reached for his daughter's hand. "Yes, we'll throw that thing away. But for now let's go see what your mama's cooking for supper." Departing the shanty, he led the way across the yard to his cook-shanty home.

CHAPTER 5

HANNAH HURRIED ALONG Birch Lake Road toward the gorge where her brother hid from the world. She slipped over the bank and made her way into the chasm. There she found Seth sitting on a log near the old shack. A couple of small crappies roasted over the dying embers of a campfire nearby.

"How do you like my fire pit?" Seth asked as she came near. "Looks good," Hannah responded. "I see you're making yourself a real home around here."

A dark cloud spread across Seth's face, but it was quickly replaced with a smile. "Well, as long as I gotta stay here, I might as well fix it up."

Hannah felt a tug on her heartstrings. Why couldn't Seth come home with her? There was no reason to scrounge around like this for food. But she held her tongue. "I'll look around," she said, "and see if I can find some traps."

Seth's brow shot upward. "That sounds good, but won't they notice if you go dragging tools and stuff away from the place?"

"I don't think so," Hannah responded. "Clive set a bunch of traps the other day, and if there are any left, it's because he

21

doesn't know they're there."

The young man leaned forward, turning the fish over in the fire. "Who's Clive?"

"Oh, that's right. You don't know Clive. He's Katherine's new husband. She married him after Pa died."

"Well, it would be nice to have some traps, but don't get yourself in trouble."

"Don't worry about me," Hannah responded. "I'll be careful." She took a seat on the log beside her brother and asked the question that had been on her mind since he arrived. "By the way, what would happen if you were caught? Would you have to go back to Canada?"

Seth turned away. "I can't talk about it."

"Why?" Hannah paused before continuing, "What have you done that's so awful?"

"I just can't talk about it."

Without warning Wolf burst from under the trees. He ran straight to Seth, crawling onto the young man's lap with his hind feet on the ground and his head and shoulders in Seth's face.

Seth stroked the dog's neck and ears, reached for a stick and tossed it across the way. "Fetch," he commanded, and Wolf raced after it.

"Looks like you two are getting along pretty well," Hannah remarked.

Seth grinned, turning the fish as he spoke. "Yes, he comes by every now and then. We hang around together, doing whatever comes to mind."

Wolf secured the stick and carried it back to his friend, only to be sent chasing after it again.

"You always did have a way with animals," Hannah said. "Do you remember how old Ted used to crawl onto your bed the minute you blew out the lights?"

"Yes, old Ted was a great bed warmer. I just moved over and made room for him. Sometimes I even let him under the blankets.

Hannah laughed as she remembered her grandmother complaining about the dirty paw marks on the bedding. "Whatever happened to old Ted?"

Seth's face transformed into a reminiscent smile. "He finally just got old and went off behind the barn to die."

Hannah and her brother talked of Grandma and Grandpa McLean and life on the farm. They talked of good times playing in the hay and rolling down Parish Hill in a barrel. They spoke of campfires under the evergreens and the tire swing that hung from the big oak tree in the backyard.

Several times Hannah tried to broach the subject of the intrusive stranger, but Seth evaded the subject. It was obvious he wanted nothing to do with the matter.

Finally Hannah left without saying a word about the disturbing young man who so troubled her.

Katherine bent, dug a hole in the soft dark earth, and dropped a tomato plant into it. Then she packed it with rich, moist soil and reached for another seedling. A gentle glow overspread her soul as she considered her future with her husband and her family. One day this land would be a thriving farm where they would live happily ever after.

Suddenly a voice broke out of nowhere. "Where's Clive?"

Looking up, Katherine saw Al Weaver, standing akimbo with a scowl on his face. "He's in the men's shanty," she said. "Why?" Al Weaver stormed across the yard without another word.

Immediately Al's wife, Verna, appeared around the corner of the house with their son, Bobby.

Katherine rose, brushed the dirt off her apron and went to meet them. "Well, what's got him by the tail?" she wanted to know.

"There's a sick fox out there somewhere," Verna said. "He was hangin' around our place last night, staggering and drooling all over everything. Al was so mad he just about had a heart attack."

"He was around here the other day too," Katherine said. "Clive went after him but he didn't succeed, so he went out the next day and set traps."

"Well, something's gotta be done before he sickens the whole community, and Al's determined to do it."

Then Al and Clive came walking around the barn with Faith Ann alongside. "Now we'll have to shoot poor Fi," Al spat.

Tears welled in Bobby's eyes. "Fi got bit, and Pa's really mad. He says we gotta kill Fi."

Verna cast a pleading glance at Al. "Can't we just pen her up for a while? We didn't see any confrontation, and we don't know for sure. At least we ought to give the dog a chance."

"I don't think so." The man pointed his finger at no one in particular. "Rabies is nothing to fool with."

"But what if you're wrong? What if it's not rabies, and you kill that dog for no reason?"

"It's rabies, all right," Al said. "I know rabies when I see it." Tears flowed down Bobby's cheeks, and Faith Ann moved close.

"I'm sorry, Bobby," she said. "Maybe I can share Wolf with you."

"Oh, all right." Al's lips pursed into a thin line. "We'll keep her in a pen for a few weeks, but I'm tellin' you, she'll get the rabies and we'll have to shoot her."

Relief overspread Verna's face. "Thank you, Al," she said. Bobby wiped the tears from his face, leaving blackened streaks across his cheeks. "Thanks, Pa."

Several weeks later Hannah, Katherine, and Faith Ann walked along Birch Lake Road toward Hitchcock's Store.

"What have you heard about Fi?" Hannah asked. "Did she ever come down with rabies?"

"Haven't heard a word," Katherine responded. "But if she's not sick yet, she should be okay."

"Well, I hope so. It would just about kill poor Bobby if his dog had to be put down."

As they came near the dog raced across the yard, smashing into Faith Ann and wagging her entire backside.

Faith Ann pushed at Fi, trying to escape her kisses, but the dog just slobbered all the more.

"Down, Fi," Hannah yelled—but Fi paid no attention.

Then the door opened, and Verna appeared with young Bobby close behind. "Down, Fi," Verna yelled. She clapped her hands with a loud and commanding slap, and the dog dropped onto all fours, hanging her head and pulling her tail between her legs. "It's okay," Verna said. "The vet says she's okay, so we released her several days ago."

A warm glow filled Hannah's heart. Not only had Bobby's pet failed to contract the illness, but she had also escaped death at her master's hand. The young woman stood waiting, shifting from one foot to another, as Katherine and Verna visited.

After several long minutes, Katherine pronounced it time to go, but she continued to chat.

Hannah leaned on one foot and then the other. She looked up at the treetops and studied the flutter of the leaves in the breeze. She drew mental pictures of flowers along the pathway. She gazed around, looking for some sign of Faith Ann and Bobby.

"Faith Ann," Katherine called at last, "c'mere!"

Faith Ann came running and the family continued on their way to the store.

Fifteen minutes later, the ladies arrived at Hitchcock's General Store. They stepped inside, and Hannah's blood turned to ice. There behind the counter stood the stranger who'd been hanging around asking questions.

"Hello, ladies," Sam said. "I'd like you to meet Adam Beste." He clapped the young man on the back, grinning from ear to ear. "Adam came over from Ontario a week or so ago and has agreed to clerk for me."

Instantly a pool of turmoil welled in Hannah's stomach. That nosy man would be at the center of everything in the village. She turned toward the bookshelf, studying the titles and staying as far away from Adam Beste as possible.

It wasn't long, however, before she felt a presence close behind her. "May I help you?"

Hannah's jaw tensed. She stared at the magazines without speaking.

"They tell me you come from Canada," he said.

"Yes." Hannah gritted her teeth and mumbled her response.

"I'm Canadian too," he continued. "Maybe we could get together sometime. I'd like to get to know the folks around here." Hannah sighed and walked away, leaving Adam Beste standing.

She looked at Katherine, who was poring over a shelf of fabrics. *For crying out loud*, Katherine, *let's get out of here.* Hannah's heart screamed its frustration, but her lips remained silent.

Katherine stood unmoving, mulling over the stock.

Finally, an eternity later, Hannah's stepmother moved to the counter. "Sam," she said, "we're going over to Uncle Ned's place, and we'd like to pick up their mail along with ours."

Sam reached into the box, sorted through the letters, and handed several to Katherine. Katherine accepted the pack and turned toward the exit.

Outside, Katherine thumbed through the posts and found her own mail. "Look," she said, "a letter from Grandma and Grandpa McLean." She tore it open and read it aloud.

> *Dear Katherine and all,*
>
> *How are you? Grandpa and I are okay. We are in good health, and we have all the provisions we need, but we're concerned about Seth. He went out shooting crows one day with a friend and never returned. We're worried sick. If he comes that way, please let us know.*
> *Ma and Pa McLean*

Hannah cringed. Seth was missing, and she knew where he was. How long could she live in this world of subterfuge and deception, knowing about her brother's presence and saying nothing? She walked on, wishing for a release from her promise.

CHAPTER 6

WHEN HANNAH HADN'T found traps in the barn, Seth decided to build his own snare. The device was a square cage made of sticks bound together with vines. It had a gate that would fall into place after an animal entered. He checked each connection for strength, tested the hatch, and then peered around the gulch, looking for a likely place to trap a rabbit. As he stood examining his creation, a rustling sound in the underbrush caught his attention. He cocked his ear and held his breath, listening until the spent air in his lungs escaped unbidden. The only sounds were the twitter of birds and the whir of the breeze in the treetops.

Then he saw it—a fox, standing in the underbrush. Its glassy eyes pierced the atmosphere and spittle dripped from its jaw. It stared at him in a murderous haze. Foam spread across its lips, and it trembled with crazed fury.

Terror quivered in Seth's gut. He stood face to face with the beast, frozen in time.

The animal charged, targeting Seth's torso with his beady, incensed eyes and Seth hurled the cage smashing him full in the face and breaking his onslaught. The fox hesitated, trembling and slavering at the mouth.

"God help me," the young man cried.

In a flash, Wolf burst from the trees. He lunged at the fox, growling and biting, and tearing at the intruder's flesh.

"Wolf, no," Seth shouted, but he may as well have yelled at the wind, for the combatants paid no heed. The fox let out a frenzied bleat, clawing at Seth's friend with wild-eyed abandon. Wolf responded in a fury of blood and teeth, wrestling his enemy to the ground, snapping and clawing and chewing. Flesh tore at flesh, and blood flew.

Finally Wolf caught the animal's neck in his jaw. He clamped down hard, lifting his adversary into the air, flinging him around and smashing him onto the ground.

And the fox went limp.

Wolf dropped his foe and stumbled toward the hill, torn and bleeding.

Tears flowed freely for a friend who would surely die.

"Now what, Seth?" Hannah's voice sounded behind him, hollow and void. "Will you come home with me and see the family?"

"No, I can't come home with you, not now and not ever. In fact, I'll have to leave the area entirely. They'll come looking for the animal that chewed up Wolf's hide, and I can't let them find me here."

Tears broke from Hannah's eyes. "Please, Seth, come home with me. You'll be welcomed with open arms. Everyone will be overjoyed to see you."

But Seth stood firm. "I can't come home with you. I'll let you know where I am as soon as I can." He stripped the case from his pillow, strung a rope through its hem and gathered his fish line and hooks. He stuffed them in the bag along with a knife, some matches, a washcloth, a towel, and soap. Soon the young man had a pack much like the "turkeys" the lumberjacks carried. Together the siblings folded Katherine's blanket, and Hannah picked up the pillow and other recognizable items.

Then Seth lifted his turkey and slung it over his shoulder, and the two siblings climbed the wall of the canyon.

They stood at the crest, dreading the moment when they would part. "Seth," Hannah whispered, "don't be gone forever. Come back as soon as you can."

"I will, Hannah. I will." Brother and sister stood gazing into one another's eyes, hardly daring to breathe lest they should lose contact.

Finally Seth pulled his sister into an embrace. He said his goodbyes and headed north, away from the village where his people lived, and into the deep woods.

Hannah trudged down Birch Lake Road with tears streaming from her eyes. She'd lost her brother again, just when she had reestablished a kinship with him. She clamped her eyes shut, trying to stop the flood of pain, but the misery in her heart would not be denied. She dropped onto a stump near Torrie's Spring and wept until her lungs hurt. What was left for her? Would she never belong with anyone?

After many minutes of uncontrollable sobbing and with spasms of grief-borne nausea churning in her stomach, she reached for the old tin cup that hung on a branch nearby and drank her fill. Then she carried the blanket and things to Torrie's old red barn and made her way back toward Camp 8.

On arrival, she entered her home with eyes that burned with pain.

Katherine looked up. "Hannah, are you all right?"

"I'm okay," Hannah said, but the trembling in her voice belied her statement, and she knew it.

"You look like you'd just been ripped apart by some monumental upheaval."

"Well, I guess I was." Hannah turned her back to hide her emotions. "It's Grandma McLean's letter," she lied. "I can't get it out of my mind. Sometimes I get to thinking God hates me. He took my ma, he took my pa, and now he has taken Seth." The truth passed her lips like a bitter herb.

"Oh Hannah, don't imagine that God hates you. It doesn't get you anywhere. That's what I thought for such a long time, and it only leads to pain."

Nevertheless, Hannah couldn't help but wonder. She walked behind the coatroom wall and flopped onto her bed, feeling empty and deserted.

Clive dipped his shovel into the dirty, tobacco be-grimed sand in the spit-box and tossed it into the wheelbarrow. When the handcart was full, he transported the mess outside and across the field to the tree line. There he tipped the load onto the ground and turned back toward the building that would one day become his tool shed. Then as he came near the cook shanty, a thunderbolt crashed through his chest. There in front of him was Wolf, torn and bloody.

He dropped the wheelbarrow and raced toward his friend.

But he stopped short. Wolf fell at his feet—dead.

In an instant Faith Ann burst from the cook shanty with Katherine close behind, "Wolf!" the young girl hollered. "Wolf, what's wrong with you?" She dashed toward the dog, screaming at the top of her lungs.

"No, Faith Ann!" Clive caught the girl by the arm and pulled her away. "Wolf has been in a fight. We don't know what happened, but we do know there's at least one rabid animal out there. You mustn't touch him."

Faith Ann leaned against her father's side, trembling at the sight of her dead pet's body.

Then Clive reached down and pulled her close, trying to ease her pain. This was his daughter—truly his daughter—and he loved her deeply.

Clive turned to Katherine. "Why don't you take Faith Ann inside?" he said. "And I'll take care of Wolf."

Faith Ann's face twisted into a grimace. "What are you going to do?"

"Well, honey, I guess I'll take him out back and find a nice place for him to rest."

Katherine reached for Faith Ann's hand and the girl followed her mother, peering sidelong at Clive, who headed for the men's shanty and a shovel. He scooped the dog into the wheelbarrow and headed toward the woods.

When the burial was finished, Clive returned to the bloody patch of ground where Wolf had died. A stream of red marked the path of death, and he knew what he must do. He needed to find what was out there.

With gun in hand he moved down the lane in search of evidence, hopeful that Wolf had not died in vain—that if Clive's dog had to die, at least he'd done away with that rabid fox.

As he walked, he passed Torrie's Spring, taking note of the tin cup that hung on a limb nearby. The flow was a community well and the cup a shared convenience. Anyone who came by might stop to refresh him or herself with the sparkling fresh water that spewed from the fount. He grabbed a quick drink and continued on his way.

Keeping his eye on the bloodstained soil, he continued down the road until he reached the gulch at Little Birch Lake. There the path turned and headed into the brush. Clive gritted his teeth and proceeded into the ravine. As he reached the floor of the gorge, he fell back. The dilapidated old shanty he had expected to find had been refurbished. The hinges on the door were secured, the leather hasp had been repaired, and there was a fire pit near the entrance. The grass and weeds around the hut were matted and flat where they had been walked over many times. Someone had been living in the gulch.

Looking around, Clive saw what he had come for—a battle ground, spattered with blood and fur, and in its midst lay the body of a fox—smashed and broken. This was the animal that had killed Clive's dog. It was misshapen, matted with blood, and rabid. He went home for his shovel and returned to dig a hole. Then he scooped the beast into the cavity and covered it with soil. The community didn't need a host of small animals feeding on its flesh.

Seth walked through the woods in the early dusk, weary and worn. Crickets chirped, owls hooted, and mosquitoes buzzed around his head. Exhaustion filled his bones after walking all day. He'd had little to eat and only a small jar of water that he'd scooped from a river as he passed by. Daylight ebbed, and yet he walked. He had to find a place to spend the night. *I'll be a fugitive for the rest of my life*, he thought.

At last an opening appeared in the trees, and he moved toward it, coming shortly to a clearing. A house stood in the distance with its form veiled in shades of night and a flickering of lamplight shining through its windows. The light appeared to be moving from one place to another, illuminating an area, only to recede and grow dark as another area brightened. Then the glow settled near the rear of the building. It appeared to be resting on a table or a stand. Soon a hazy figure came into view through the curtain, a woman most likely, for she wore a loose gown and a nightcap over her head. She hovered near the lamp and darkness filled the night. The family had gone to bed.

A barn stood in the yard, and Seth decided to bed down in the straw. He'd talk to the farmer tomorrow.

Dog-tired, the young man entered the building and dropped onto a pile of hay with his turkey by his side. Within minutes his weary bones took control, and he plummeted into dreamless oblivion.

The next thing Seth knew, he was jarred awake by a balding old man with wrinkled overalls and a snarl on his face. "What are you doing in my barn?" The man glared down at Seth with a pitchfork in his hand and a scowl on his face. "I come out here to feed my cows and what do I find, but a hooligan lying on my hay."

A knot rose in the Seth's throat. "I didn't mean any harm, mister," he stammered. "I'd been walking all day without much to eat or drink and . . . I just took a little shelter for the night."

"So who are you; and what're you doing here?"

"My name is Jeb, Jeb Farley." Seth said the first thing that came to mind. He didn't know where it came from, but it fit the need. "I'm looking for work and a place to stay for a while."

The man stood the pitchfork on the floor, holding it by the handle. "I'm Tim Bronson," he said. "I suppose you could stay for a few days, if you want to help out with the chores."

Seth's heart beat fast. "That would be really kind of you, mister."

"Well then, let's go to the house and you can meet my wife and eat breakfast."

Seth followed the farmer to a small lean-to back shed with a dirt floor and roughly fashioned steps. Following the farmer's lead, he took off his jacket and hung it on a nail. Then he and Tim Bronson entered through a kitchen door.

"Mary," Tim Bronson called as they stepped inside. "I found this fellow sleeping in the barn. His name's Jeb Farley and he says he wants to work, so I agreed to let him stay for few days."

"Well, young man," Mary Bronson said, "come on in. I'll set a place for you." Mary led the way to the table, and Seth took a seat, overtaken with thankfulness to be sitting at a real table with real food and a family for company.

CHAPTER 7

I T WAS THE strangest thing," Clive said. He helped himself to a slice of bread, spread a thick layer of butter on it, and laid it on his plate. "The door had been repaired and there was a newly built fire pit in front of it. It was as if someone had been living there recently."

Katherine looked up. "Do you think there might be a crook of some kind out there?"

"Oh, I don't think so," Clive responded. "Probably just some hobo taking shelter." He selected a boiled potato, mashed it with his fork, and covered it with brown gravy, a condiment that was made of flour fried in grease until it turned brown and then thinned with water.

"Well, anyway, that rabid fox is gone," Katherine said.

Clive took a deep breath. "And I should go tell the Weavers about it."

Faith Ann's eyes lit up with hope. "Can I go too, Mister Clive?"

"Why don't we all go?" Katherine said. "We can tell them about the fox and do a little visiting."

"Good idea," Clive responded.

"And you can bring your harmonica. Maybe they'll be in the mood for some music."

"We'll do it after supper," Clive said. He rose to his feet and made his way to the door. "Right now I gotta get that shelf nailed in the tool shed wall."

Later that evening the Isamans climbed into the buggy and headed for the neighbors' farm. It was a short ride, and as they pulled into the drive, Fi came barreling out to meet them. Bobby followed close behind.

"C'mon out back," the boy hollered. "We got baby chicks."

Faith Ann jumped onto the ground and followed her friend toward the backyard and an evening of fun and games. The rest of the family moved toward the front porch. As they came near, the door opened, and Al Weaver stepped outside. "Hey Verna," he called. "We got company; the Isamans are here."

Verna appeared in the doorway all smiles and ready for some good neighborly gossip. "Come on in," she said. "I have bread coming out of the oven in about five minutes. We'll have fresh hot rolls and coffee." The ladies made their way to the kitchen, while Al and Clive retired to the sitting room.

"So, what's going on with you folks?" Al asked.

"Good news," Clive responded. "That rabid fox is dead."

Al's eyebrows lifted. "Great! How do you know?"

"I found him out at Little Birch Lake, ripped to shreds and deader'n a doornail." Clive brushed his hand over his chin. "Actually it was Wolf that got him," he said.

"Oh?"

"Apparently the fox and Wolf got into a fight." Clive went over the afternoon's events, including Wolf's death and the trail of blood. "And I buried the fox right then and there. We don't need a bunch of wild animals feeding on his flesh."

"Good job." Al slapped his knee and changed the subject. "So, how's the farming going?"

"Well, I got the potatoes in and ..." Suddenly the door opened and Faith Ann came rushing in with Bobby close behind. "Mr. Clive, Mr. Clive."

Clive turned.

"Bobby says Fi's gonna have puppies and maybe Wolf's the pa."

"How about that?" Clive grinned at the joy on his daughter's face.

"Can I have one?" she went on. "Can I? Can I?"

"You bet," Clive said. "In fact, when they're ready, we'll come over, and you can pick the one you like."

A shadow crossed Faith Ann's face and was quickly replaced with a smile. "I'm sorry Wolf died," she said, "but it'll be okay 'cause we're gonna get one of his babies." With that, the children turned and ran out the door, returning to their own little world.

That evening, as the neighbors sat visiting, Al picked up his guitar and began to strum a tune. As if in sync, Clive whipped out his harmonica and brushed it past his lips. Soon everyone joined the fun, and the household rang with music. Then when the sun sank in the west and the world grew dark, the Isamans said their goodbyes and returned home.

Later that night Clive and Katherine lay resting in their bed when Katherine leaned close. "Clive," she whispered, "I have something to tell you."

Clive's heart skipped a beat. What might Katherine have to say that would generate such reverence?

She reached for his hand and laid it across her midsection. "Do you feel movement?" She paused and then went on. "That's your child," she said. "We're going to have a baby."

"What? Are you sure?"

"I'm sure, and Granny Weemes says it's due in December."

Clive turned and held his wife close. "I love you," he said. "And this time I'll be here to welcome our child."

Seth bent, picked up a rock, and tossed it onto the stone boat. Then, he and Tim Bronson followed the horses toward the pile of stones at the edge of the field. There he and Tim emptied the flatbed one rock at time.

"Okay, boys, let's go home," Tim called. He flicked the reins, and the horses took off at a trot. It had been a long day, and both men and horses were tired.

"Well, how about that?" Tim Bronson said as they came near the barn. "There's Sheriff Munson. What do you suppose he wants with us?"

Seth's heart did a double take. If there was anything Seth didn't need, it was the law hanging around, interfering in his life. He stepped back, wishing he could walk away, but it wasn't possible. He followed his host toward the sheriff's vehicle.

"Well, Brandt," Tim Bronson said as the sheriff drew his transport to a stop. "What're you doing out here in this neck of the woods?"

"Just kind of scoutin' the countryside," the sheriff drawled.

The man hopped onto the ground and stood visiting while Seth fidgeted in his boots.

"Well, come on in and sit fer a spell," Tim said.

"Better not," Brandt responded. "Bessie'll have supper ready, and you know how women are. They like you to come in on time."

"Oh, well, don't say I didn't offer."

The sheriff nodded in Seth's direction. "So, who's your new friend?"

"Jeb Farley," Tim Bronson responded. "He came by a while ago on his way to the Upper Peninsula. Said he needed a little break, so I took him on for a few days."

"Nice to meet you, young man," the sheriff said.

"Nice to meet you too, Sheriff," Seth responded. His eyes scanned the area, seeking an escape. Then he noticed the outhouse standing behind the woodshed. "Excuse me, sir," he said. "I need to make a stop out back." He offered an improvised smile and walked away.

Reaching the privy, Seth collapsed on the seat, gulping to control the nauseous tremors in his stomach. He buried his face in his hands and wept dry tears. Now he'd have to leave the Bronsons' farm and head back into the woods.

When his nerves were under control, he noticed a copy of the *Police Gazette* lying on the floor. Several pages had been torn loose and he thumbed through the remaining leaves until a headline caught his eye.

Sheriff Invites Lumberjack to Leave Town

In an early morning meeting, it is said that Sheriff Payne was seen talking in a bar with Big Jack Mackie, the lumberjack who's been terrorizing the west side. "If he were to leave town," the sheriff is said to have commented, "I'd just let him go and never bother him again."

The wheels in Seth's head began to turn. He could just disappear into the deep woods, where he could lose himself forever, and with the invention of the logging wheels, some of the jacks were now working in the summer. He tore the page from the magazine, folded it, and stuffed it in his pocket.

Clive stood in the men's shanty, holding a board he'd just ripped from a bunk, when a voice called from the doorway.

"Hello, is anyone around? Your wife said I could come out here and talk to you."

"Yes, what do you want?" Clive put down the board and approached Adam Beste.

"Do you remember me? I've been working for Sam Hitchcock for about a week now."

"Yes," Clive responded. "Sam says you're good at ciphering and you make a fine clerk."

"Well, I've been staying with Sam, but there's really not room for me there. He said you might have a cot here in the men's shanty that I could rent for a few weeks."

Clive stepped back in surprise. "Well, it's not something I'd put a lot of thought into."

"I wouldn't need much space, and there doesn't seem to be a room available anywhere in the area." Adam pointed toward the far corner. "That bed over there would be fine; I'd pay you fifty cents a week, and I could even help with chores and stuff."

"I don't know." Clive put down the pry bar he'd been using and moved toward the door. He led the way outside, observing the young man's tall lean stature and his generally pleasant appearance. "I have to say, it'd be kind of nice to have another man around the place, but I'd better talk with my wife about it."

That night after supper, Clive approached Katherine. "He's willing to pay fifty cents a week and help with the chores. Fifty cents a week would come in mighty handy."

Katherine shook her head. "I don't know."

"He said he'd sleep in a corner of the men's shanty, and I guess it wouldn't interfere with things too much. I could finish the remodeling when he's gone."

"Well, it's your space. Whatever you do with it is okay with me." A smile curled Clive's lips. "He said he'd be back tomorrow, and I'll tell him he can stay.

The next day Katherine stood in the kitchen, doing the weekly ironing. She'd sprinkled the clothes the day before and they were perfectly moist and ready. Soon the iron grew cool and she put it onto the range, picking up the hot one that sat warming there. She unrolled a shirt, laid the collar on the board, and pressed it flat. Then as she laid out a sleeve, Faith Ann came inside with Bobby Weaver. "Fi's got babies," the girl announced, "and Mr. Clive said I could have one. Can I go over and see 'em, please?"

Katherine looked at the basket of clothes that were yet to be pressed. It would take at least another hour to finish the job.

"Not right now, sweetheart. I have to get this ironing done."

Faith Ann's face fell. "Mr. Clive said I could have a puppy, and I want to go pick him out."

"Oh, I suppose. You kids go ahead and I'll come after you when I'm finished." The two children took off at a run as Katherine smoothed the shirt over the ironing board.

Later, Katherine made her way across the field to the Weaver house, where she stood looking down at a squirming mass of furry flesh. The eyes weren't open yet, and it would be several weeks before the puppies were ready to leave their mother, but Faith Ann had already chosen her own. "This one's mine," she said, pointing to a little female with a white face and a spattering of white on her chest. "And I can have her as soon as she gets big enough." Faith Ann's eyes sparkled. "I gave her a name already. Her name is Sassy."

Katherine grinned at Verna Weaver, sharing a moment of intimacy as their children bonded with the wriggling, squirming mass. Then Verna turned. "C'mon inside," she said. "Let's have coffee before you go."

CHAPTER 8

SETH SAT IN the outhouse waiting for Sheriff Munson to leave. He could hear voices outside, and he leaned forward, listening. "It's been good talking with you, Tim," the sheriff said. "I'd like to stay longer, but Bessie's waiting, you know."

"Too bad you didn't get a chance to visit with Jeb while you were here," Tim said. "He's a good man, and you'd like him."

Seth peeked through a crack in the wall to see the sheriff climb into his buggy.

"Well, maybe I'll see him the next time I come by." The sheriff flicked the reins, and the buggy began to move. The wheels creaked, and hoof beats marked a steady rhythm on the road.

Seth exited the privy, walking slowly to allow plenty of time for Sheriff Munson to make a complete departure.

"Too bad you weren't a little quicker," Tim Bronson said as he came near. "The sheriff just left."

Seth's insides shuddered. He had to get out of here.

"He indicated he'd be back before too long though," Tim went on, "and he'd like to get to know you. I'm sure you'd like him."

Oh well, so much for shelter at the Bronsons' farm.

Just then, the front door opened, and Mary Bronson appeared in the entryway. "Hey, you two, supper's getting cold."

"Okay, we're coming," Tim called. He and Seth moved toward the house. They entered the kitchen and washed their hands in a basin of warm water that had been drawn from the reservoir. They wiped on a ragged towel and took their places at the table.

As they dined, Seth mentioned his upcoming departure. "You know," he said. "I'm going to have to be on my way north again soon. Grandma'll be looking for me, and I do want to get there before winter sets in." It was a lie, and he hoped the Bronsons wouldn't notice the tremble in his voice.

"That's too bad," Tim responded. "I rather liked having you around."

"We'll miss you, all right," Mary said. "We never had a son, and I've kind of pretended you were my own."

"Just the same," Tim went on. "We understand, and when you're ready to leave, we'll do what we can to make your trip as easy as possible."

"Thank you," Seth said. "You folks have been really thoughtful." He breathed deeply; the parting had begun.

That night Seth went to bed with a storm brewing in his gut. Tomorrow he'd tell the Bronsons he planned to leave within the week. Then he'd prepare his "turkey" for a trek to some summer lumber camp, where he'd be away from the ever present threat of discovery.

Over the next several days, Seth worked with Tim Bronson to clear the field of rocks, and all the while he was filled with anxiety. The young man watched and waited, dreading every sunrise. What if the sheriff came back? Would he realize who he was talking to?

Finally the day of departure came. Seth stood with the Bronsons making idle conversation and passing those last melancholy moments. Mary had packed a couple of fried-egg sandwiches for his lunch, along with some radishes, carrots, and green onions from the garden. She'd included some dried beef and smoked fish for the long term and a small bag of dried apple slices. Add to that the batch of sugar cookies she'd made for a treat along the way, and Seth was well-prepared for the departure.

Tim found an old tin cup in the tool shed, and Seth stuffed it into the pillowcase with the food. A cup could come in mighty handy as he traveled.

Then at last the young man headed down the lane, he knew not where. Looking back, Seth could see tears in Mary's eyes.

"Maybe I'll come back to visit sometime," he called.

"Maybe," Tim responded, but both Seth and the Bronsons knew it wasn't likely.

"Anyway, thank you for all you've done." Seth waved good-bye and walked away.

"Hannah, take this bedding out to the men's shanty and make the bed for Mr. Beste." Katherine pointed to a stack of sheets and blankets that lay on the table. "He'll be using the bunk in the far corner. The tick's already on it."

Hannah scowled. "I don't see why we have to accommodate that man. He's an intruder in town, and we don't know anything about him." She took the blankets and headed out the door.

"And by the way," Katherine went on, "have you seen that crazy-quilt that was in the cedar chest? It's disappeared, and I don't know where it went."

Hannah didn't answer. She guessed she'd better go get that stuff she left in Torrie's barn—and she'd better do it soon. She turned toward the door to escape further questions.

In the men's shanty, Hannah heaved the covers at the bed. "There, Adam Beste. There's your lousy bedding." Nevertheless, she knew she had a job to do, so she flung a sheet around the tick and yanked the quilts over it. Then she left the building, smoldering with indignation. Why didn't that man just go back where he came from? What was he doing, poking around in people's business anyway? Well, he'd better stay away from Hannah, because she wasn't about to get close with any nosy intruder from Canada.

Several hours later, as the sun fell below the trees and the sky filled with the pinkish glow of evening, Hannah sat in the swing under the buckeye tree. She took in the music of the crickets singing to the moon and the glint of the fireflies with their tiny lights flickering in the night. She wondered about her brother. What was he doing on that warm and balmy evening? She hoped he was well and that he was enjoying the stillness of the twilight. It was a precious time, and she reveled in the serenity of it all.

Then her moment of bliss was translated into vexation. Adam Beste came near. He leaned against the big horse chestnut tree with his arms folded across his chest. "It's a beautiful evening, isn't it?" he said.

"Yes, I guess so." Hannah gritted her teeth and muttered the words into the mist. *At least it was until you came along.*

"It certainly is nice of your folks to let me stay here."

"Yeah, I guess so."

"It's good to be close by like this, so I can get to know your family. I'm new around here, you know."

"Yes, I noticed." Although Hannah's antipathy resounded in her voice, the young man didn't seem to notice. He stood passing the time of day until Hannah thought she'd scream.

Finally, he walked away, and the young woman let out a sigh of relief, pushing the swing into motion. Why had Clive agreed to let that interloper hang around?

Clive stood erect with hands on hips, stretching to ease the pressure on his back. He'd been digging around that old stump for weeks, and when he wasn't digging, he was chopping at root stems and trying to free the stub so the horses could pull it loose. He removed his cap and stood scratching his head, looking at the stub and mentally calculating the work at hand. Noticing an uncut shoot, he stepped back into the hole and chopped at it. Then he stood for several seconds, examining his work. Brushing his arm against his forehead, he bent down to pull the dirt away from the root, and there, entangled in the rootstock, was a rock—a rock that was big enough to scare a dinosaur. "Oh, rats," he spat. He bent, pulled the dirt away from the base, and took on the incredible task of freeing the stump from the stone.

Time passed, evening fell, and Clive picked up his tools and headed toward the men's shanty. As he stepped inside, he noticed the movable wall he'd built to give Adam Beste some privacy. He rather liked the idea of the young man's presence on the place.

He hung his axe on a couple of nails he'd driven into the west wall and put the shovel in a corner. Then he exited the building and headed for the cook shanty.

Inside, the aroma of fresh, hot johnnycake filled the air, and a pot of bean soup simmered on the range. Katherine was reaching for a ladle, and Hannah and Faith Ann were setting the table.

"It sure smells good in here," Clive sang.

As he spoke, he looked up at Hannah's countenance. The girl wore a perpetual frown these days, and for some reason that he did not quite understand, she really disliked Adam Beste. The young man treated her with utmost consideration, and he was likeable enough, but Hannah would have nothing to do with him. Clive shook his head in frustration. That girl should give the young man a chance.

Then as he took his place at the table, it occurred to him that one day he might invite Adam to join the family for meals. For now, though, the fellow seemed content to take his food with Sam Hitchcock, and Hannah was so antagonistic toward him that it would make dinner miserable if he ate with them.

After supper the ladies cleared the table and did the dishes while Clive sat on the settee reading the *Police Gazette*. It had been a hard day, and he planned to coast into the evening with his magazine.

CHAPTER 9

SETH'S SHOULDERS HUNG low as he trudged along an unknown path toward an unknown destination. He was tired and hungry, and he yearned for a good meal at a proper table. He closed his eyes, wishing there were some way he could undo the deeds of the past. How could he have come so far from his roots?

In time the young man came to a rise in the terrain where the ripple of flowing waters seeped into his consciousness. He turned and made his way over the edge to a downward gradient, where he stood in awe. A dozen tiny geysers spewed from the hillside, forming little waterways that gurgled over the land and gathered into streams. Then the streams flowed ever downward toward some distant goal. Seth stood for several minutes, marveling at the sweep that lay within his sight. Then he turned to follow the flow.

As he walked, the tiny waterways came together to form a rippling brook. Crystal-clear waters surged over a bed of golden sand that shifted and spiraled in undulating curves and swells. This, he decided, was a good place to eat his lunch. He filled his tin cup with water from the stream, found an old stump for a seat, and rummaged through his supplies. Selecting some of Mary's dried beef and carrots, he dined in nature's café, finishing with the last of his sugar cookies. Then, with the meal finished, he closed his turkey and continued on his way.

All afternoon the young man hiked, tramping over hills and swamps, past tall trees and thick underbrush until, at last, he came upon a camp huddled in the scrub. Two young boys stood in a puddle of water with their backs turned. They were mud covered and soaked to the waist.

"Hello," Seth called as he came near. "What have you got there?" The children turned. "It's a boat," the larger child responded. "Pa whittled it out for me." The boy held up the craft and Seth accepted it, turning it over in his hands and observing its carefully carved shape.

"And he's doing one for me," the other lad interjected. "He's almost done. He thinks he can finish next Sunday."

"Watch this." The first youngster retrieved his toy, put it in the water and gave it a shove. When it floated away, he chased it, caught it and sent it back, glowing with satisfaction.

"My name's Dean," said the younger of the two. "And that's my brother, Eric. What's your name?"

Seth grinned. "My name is Jeb." He repeated the name he'd given to the Bronsons. "I thought I might stay around a while and work with your folks. Is your pa at home?"

"Pa's out in the woods hauling logs," Eric said. "But our ma's over there in the cook shanty. Want to talk to her?"

"Sure." Seth followed the boys across the way and soon they came near a fairly large log building. Eric ran ahead, pulled open the door and yelled, "Hey Ma, there's someone out here to see you."

In response, a woman stepped outside. She was full figured with dark hair and had a gingham apron wrapped around her torso. Immediately, her attention settled on her sons. "What in the Sam Hill have you boys been doing?"

The youngsters looked down at their muddy pants and studied the dirt.

"Well?"

"We were playing with Eric's boat," Dean mumbled.

"Did you have to sit in the water to do it?"

A long silence ensued before Eric's voice escaped his constricted throat. "We just . . ."

"Well, get out back and clean yourselves up, before your pa gets here and catches you. Then you'll be in a peck of trouble."

The boys turned to go and the woman called after them, "And bring in some firewood when you're done. The box is almost empty."

The woman turned and her face melted into a grin. "Boys!" she said. "What are you going to do with them? I told Ike that boat'd get those kids in trouble."

Seth smiled. "Well, I seem to remember a youngster who got into trouble a time or two when he was a boy."

The woman shook her head. "I suppose boys will be boys, but mothers will be mothers too. And I don't want my kids out there soaking themselves to the gills and catching their death of foolishness." She brushed her hand over her apron. "By the way, what did you say your name is?"

"Name's Jeb—Jeb Farley."

The woman stepped back as though stunned. "Farley," she blurted. "My name is Harriet Farley. This is the Farley camp."

Seth just about collapsed. "Well, how do you like that?" he said. His mind reeled with the thought. Had he chosen a name that would get him in trouble?

"Maybe we're relatives," the woman said. "There's a bunch of us around this territory."

"Well, I just got in from Canada," Seth responded. "We have a few of 'em over there too." The admission was out before he realized the jeopardy it could bring.

"So what brings you here?" Harriet wanted to know.

"I was hoping to find a camp where I could hang around for a while. I'm on my way up north to my grand-folks' farm, and I need a break."

"Well, you'll have to talk to the men about that. They'll be along soon. In the meantime why don't you come on in and sit a spell?"

"No thank you, ma'am," Seth responded. "I'll just go around back and help the boys bring in some firewood."

"Okay," Harriet said, and she walked away.

Seth made his way around the shanty to find Eric and Dean filling their arms with split logs. "Need a little help?" he called.

"Sure," the two youngsters called in unison.

Seth filled his arms with split logs and followed the boys inside, where they dropped the fuel into a wooden crate at the end of the range and ran back outside.

"Wanna see the camp?" Eric said.

"Sure," Seth responded. He followed the boys around the site, observing the barn with smithy tools and equipment hanging on the walls. They viewed a small shack that was built on runners capable of skidding. "That's Grandpa's shanty," Dean said. "When he wants to move it, he just hooks it to the horses, and off he goes."

Seth grinned, "Pretty smart, huh?"

Just then the air was rent by the creak of moving machinery. A team of horses broke through the opening in the trees, hauling a pair of Silas Over-pack's big wheels. The device towered over the working crew with two nine-foot wagon wheels connected by an axle about a foot square.

A long tongue extended from the axle to the horses, and a man ran alongside carrying the reins. "Heave-ho," the man called and the horses plodded forward, hauling two huge logs that hung from a chain below the axle of the machine. Two men came along behind, one probably in his thirties and a younger man about Seth's age. "Whoa," the driver called at last, and the horses came to a stop near the river where an accumulation of logs had been decked.

"That's my grandpa," Dean said of the older man. "He's been in the logging camps ever since he was a little boy."

"And that's our pa and Uncle Wade," Eric went on.

The driver released the tongue from the whiffletree, and the harness. Then he pushed it upward. As the shank rose, the axle turned, and the logs dropped onto the ground between those immense wheels.

Immediately the younger men released the chain that held the timber, and the older man hauled down on the tongue. Then the bar was fastened to the whiffletree, and the men rolled away the big wheels to park them near the barn.

Dean and Eric grabbed Seth's hands and followed the men. "Grandpa," Dean called, "Grandpa, we got company."

The older man helped park the big wheels and then turned. "Well, it's nice to meet you, young man," he said. "I'm Max Farley and this is the Farley camp. What did you say your name was?"

"Name's Jeb Farley," Seth said, hoping the men would accept the lie without question.

The men burst into laughter. "Well, it's nice to meet you, Jeb Farley." The man stepped back and gestured toward his sons. "This is Ike Farley, and this is Wade Farley."

"Well, come on inside, and we'll have supper," Max Farley said.

The man turned and led the way toward the cook shanty.

As they stepped inside Harriet called out. "C'mon, you guys. Supper's ready."

The men took their places at the table, and a young woman about sixteen years old stood ready to serve. "That's my sister, Julie," Wade said as they took their places. The girl smiled through her brown eyes and brushed a long braid over her shoulder. The men dined on bean soup and johnnycake, leaving the women to eat in the kitchen later.

After supper Seth walked with Wade through the camp, observing the tree line and the river that flowed through the property. He noticed the decked logs that would one day become someone's home or cabinet or outbuilding. Seth felt at ease here. Perhaps he could remain for some time, hidden from the world.

CHAPTER 10

HANNAH STOOD OUTSIDE the tool shed waiting for Clive and fingering the straps on her stepfather's bib overalls. They hung on her like a pup tent, but it was better than a skirt for today's work. They were preparing to pull that big stump in the south field. "All you have to do," Clive had said, "is hold the board. I'll do the heavy work."

So Hannah had prepared for a day in the field, and together she and her stepfather loaded shovels and axes and pickaxes onto the buckboard.

Then Adam walked across the yard. "Do you need help?" he called.

Clive just about flew into the young man's arms. "That would be great!" he exclaimed.

The two men added a stout four-by-eight plank and a heavy chain to the load.

Hannah stood sidelined.

Finally Clive and Adam climbed aboard the wagon, Clive flicked the reins, and the carriage moved out without a thought about Hannah. She turned and made her way back across the yard, feeling empty and disregarded. "Now that interloper has taken my place," she muttered, "and I'm not needed."

"Hannah," Faith Ann came running toward her, yelling with all her might. "Can I go to the field with you?"

"I'm not going," Hannah snapped. "Adam Beste's gonna do the job."

Faith Ann's face transformed. "Hey," she sang. "Now we can go together, and you don't have to work."

Hannah stood agape; Faith Ann was right. She had escaped a lot of heavy labor at the hand of that idiot who lived in her barn. He was dumber than she thought.

With that, Hannah and Faith Ann made their way to the field, where they seated themselves on the fence row, and Hannah looked on with an icy sneer. "What luck," she mumbled. "That fool just walked right up and asked to be dumped on."

Faith Ann looked at her big sister with questioning eyes. "Hannah," She said. "What does it mean to be dumped on?"

Surprised, Hannah flicked out an answer. "Oh nothing much," she muttered. "I just mean Adam Beste gets to do a lot of hard work, and I get off scot-free."

"Mr. Beste is a nice man, don't you think?" Faith Ann said.

"Well, he sure came in handy for me just now."

Faith Ann's face twisted into a frown. "Don't you like Mr. Beste?"

Hannah's jaw stiffened. "Let's just say I don't know him very well." She completed her response with an inward slur. *And I don't want to know him either. He just wants to learn about Seth, and I'm not going to tell him anything.*

"He seems to me like a really nice person."

"Well, that depends." Hannah patted her little sister's shoulder. "Right now we want to watch Clive pull that stump." The young woman pointed toward the men. "They're just about ready."

Hannah looked up to see Adam step into the recess where he'd been digging. She grinned as she thought about her good luck to be watching instead of scrounging around in the dirt. Adam Beste might just come in handy after all.

"Hold this board upright," Clive said, as he and Adam approached the stump. "And I'll drape the chain up and over it. Then when the horses move out, it'll pull upward on the root and, hopefully, dislodge the thing."

Together the two men adjusted and twisted and moved the plank until it stood firm on solid ground. Then Clive took his place behind Blackie and Gunnar. "Giddap," he called, and the horses leaned into the harness. As they did, the links in the chain ground against one another in resistance to the load they were forced to bear. The timber twisted and turned, and the rootstock shivered and squawked—but the root refused to release its grip on the earth.

Then Adam held up a hand. "Hold it," he shouted, and the team came to rest. The young man grabbed the axe that lay nearby and jumped into the recess. He chopped at the roots, pulled back the dirt and chopped again. Finally, he tossed the axe aside, climbed out of the hole and called out. "Okay, let's try it again."

Clive plied the reins and the work began anew. "Giddap," he called and the horses gave a mighty heave. "Good boys, you can do it," Clive called, and the animals leaned in. They pulled and hauled until the flesh on their hips rippled and trembled with the effort. Then at last the stub gave way. A wrenching cacophony of splintering wood burst on the air as the rootstock broke loose.

Slowly the stump rose. It emerged from the earth with a deafening crash and tilted on its side, grounded beside its base.

The board fell to the ground and lay motionless beside the hole. "Whoa," Clive called and the horses came to a stop, their heads hung low with exhaustion. "That's all for now, boys," Clive said. "You've done a superb job. We'll dispose of that thing another day." He threw the reins over the animals' backs and patted their sides.

Finally, Clive and Adam loaded the tools onto the wagon. They tossed the plank and chain aboard the transport and took their places for the ride home. At that point Clive looked up. "C'mon, girls," he called. "You may as well ride along."

Faith Ann ran to her father and he boosted her onto the conveyance. Then, as Hannah came near, Adam held out his hand. Hannah stiffened with ire but accepted his offer.

Finally everyone was aboard, and Clive turned the team toward home. Blackie and Gunner lifted their heads, charging happily across the field.

Seth had been at the Farley camp for several weeks, and he'd pretty much settled into the routine. You rise in the morning, eat breakfast, and head for the woods. You chop branches and stack timber all morning. You clear the roadway and then hitch logs to the big wheels. Finally you head home for the evening meal and bedtime.

Just now he and Wade were preparing the last load of the day. He dragged the riser pole across the trail. Then he and Wade rolled three immense logs onto it at right angles, leaving a space between the timber and the ground. Later they would slide the canary—a long rod with a hook on the end—underneath the logs to pull the sling chain through.

At that moment, the big wheels broke through the trees. Nearer and nearer came the gigantic machine, at last it turned onto the cross-haul, a cleared pathway at right angles to the road, and came to a stop just off the main trail. Then Max pulled on the reins, and the animals backed over the logs. Slowly but precisely they crept across the forest floor until the wheels came to a stop directly over the riser pole.

Immediately Max released the tongue, sending it upward until it stood straight and tall, twelve feet in the air as if reaching for a cloud.

Then the sling chain was released from the axle, and it dropped to the ground. Seth shoved the canary through the space between the ground and the load and pulled the cable under the logs. Wade refastened the chain to the axle (the eccentric block), and Ike urged the horses forward. Down and down came the long tongue, round and round went the axle . . . and up came the logs, swinging on the chain. There they hung with one end dragging on the ground.

Finally, Max and Ike fastened the tongue to the doubletree. "Giddap," Max called, and Silas Overpack's machine lumbered through the forest with a harvest of logs hanging from its axle.

Soon the crew arrived at camp, decked the load, and took care of the horses. Then they made their way to the cook shanty, where Seth took his seat next to Wade without a word. Although the Farleys were far less strict about silence during meals than the big camps, a hush filled the air while hungry men satisfied their bodies' cravings. As each platter or bowl was emptied, Julie replaced it with a full one.

When the men finished eating, the women and children dined at the kitchen table. Tomorrow was Sunday, and the men would take a well-deserved day off.

Silas Overpack's machine was a great boon to the logging industry because it became possible to harvest the logs in summer without sleighs and ice roads to transport the logs to the mills.

CHAPTER 11

HANNAH TOOK A moment to admire her reflection in the mirror before she headed out the door. She pulled her long, honey colored hair into a knot at the back of her head and pinched her cheeks to make them a bit more rosy. "I guess you'll do," she whispered to herself.

"C'mon, it's getting late," Clive called, and Hannah grabbed a pan of baked beans, covered it with a towel, and carried it outside. She climbed into the carriage, and Clive flicked the reins. The Isamans were on their way to the annual Sunday school picnic.

Fifteen minutes later, they arrived at the grange hall, and Hannah carried the food into the building. She deposited it on the long, improvised table that ran the entire length of the community room and went to watch the outdoor activities. She made her way to the horseshoe match where her friends Mabel Porter and Polly Adkins stood watching the younger men compete. Adam Beste stepped forward, and Hannah's face twisted into a sneer. "I hope you fall on your face," she whispered to herself. "You got no business hangin' around here nosin' into everybody's business."

Meanwhile, Adam waited by the stake with the iron crescent in his hand. He stood straight and tall, eyeing the steely rod at the opposite end of the court. He lifted the horseshoe, flung it hard at the post, and the clang of iron against iron rang across the field. The missile circled its target, and Adam won the game.

Hannah's neighbors went away losers, and Hannah went away with lips curled in disgust. *Why couldn't that interloper just go home to Canada, where he belonged? I bet Seth could beat him.*

But Polly and Mabel had no such thoughts. "What do you think of that new guy?" Mabel said. "Isn't he just a taste of heaven?"

"For sure," Polly returned. "He's so good looking he makes my head spin."

"I don't know what everyone sees in that jug head," Hannah sputtered. "He just drops into the area and takes over the town. Everybody stands around like idiots and lets him get away with it." Polly's eyes grew wide.

"Hannah, how can you say that? Adam Beste is just about the best thing that's happened in this place since Hitchcock's Store brought the *Boyne City News* to town."

Hannah shrugged. "Well, he's not parked in your backyard."

"He can come to my backyard any time he wants."

Just then, the dinner bell rang and everyone went inside. There, Pastor Tibbs gave thanks, and a line formed at the serving counter. There were escalloped potatoes, deviled eggs, and fried chicken. There were bowls of potato salad decorated with radish-tulips and egg-slice-daisies, completed with cucumber slices and green onion stalks. It was a feast of feasts. Everyone ate their fill and then some.

When the meal was over, Frank Barber stood near the entry and called out to the crowd. "All right, everyone. Let's go to the recreation area. The games are about to begin." In nothing flat the children ran out the door, pushing and shoving and creating pandemonium.

"Slow down," Frank's wife, Zelda, snapped. "You can't play

games unless you know what games you're gonna play." The kids settled down to a minor riot.

Then little Betsy Funk bumped into Jake Roddick, and Jake turned with a jerk. He shoved the girl onto the ground, and Betsy began to whimper. Zelda grabbed Jake's arm and yanked the boy to attention, staring willfully into his eyes. "I said, calm down," she barked.

The boy glared at Zelda, pulling against her grip and resisting arrest, but the disciplinarian held tight—and though the youngster pulled and tugged and wrenched, he stood in place.

"We'll begin with the three-legged race," Frank called, and the children gathered around. "First you'll need to find a partner."

Faith Ann ran to Bobby Weaver. "C'mon, Bobby, we'll beat 'em all," she said. Bobby agreed, and together they ran to the starting line. Soon all the children stood ready and waiting for the race to begin—all the children, that is, except Austin Barnes, who had a mental impairment. Austin stood on the sidelines looking lost and alone.

Suddenly a cheer reverberated across the crowd, as Mac Preston, Austin's Sunday school teacher, bounded onto the field. "I found my partner," he called, and the young boy's face transformed into pure delight.

Minutes later Frank held the cowbell aloft. "Ready . . . set . . . go!" he called. He shook the bell, and it clattered like a train wreck, sending racers across the field in a dash toward possible victory.

"Go, Bobby!" Al Weaver shouted as the teams staggered down the field.

"C'mon, Faith Ann!" Katherine and Hannah called together.

"Run, Bobby!" Verna yelled, and the duo forged into first place, stumbling along with their legs tied and with the second place team only inches behind.

"Run, Bobby and Faith Ann!" Clive called, and they put on a burst of speed.

Then they tripped. In a flash Mac lifted Austin off the ground and leapt over the finish line. The town's least likely child had taken the prize.

"Frank held Austin's arms high. "The winner!" he called and the boy's eyes shone like diamonds in the sun.

But Faith Ann's eyes glistened for another reason. Tears budded and ran down her cheeks. "It's not fair," she cried. "We ran the fastest. We were winning."

Hannah knelt close to her sister. She put one arm around the girl and the other around her neighbor. "Think about this," she whispered. "Austin never comes in first at anything. Maybe it was his turn."

"Well . . . maybe," Bobby said. "But I like to win better."

Faith Ann's lips twisted into a pout. "I wanted to beat. We ran the fastest."

"It'll be okay," Hannah whispered. "Maybe you can do it next time." She untied the children's legs and walked with them to the next event, the annual ballgame between the men and the teenage boys.

Al Morris and Jim Birch were warming up on the ball field as the crowd flocked to the sidelines. The men had won last year, and everyone was anticipating a hard-fought match. "Let the event begin," Frank called. He tossed the bat to Al Morris, who caught it with one hand. Then Al Junior placed his hand above his father's, and they measured it hand over hand, until the younger man held the bat at the top. The air was rent with a shout as the boys raced for the bench and the men took their places on the field.

Al Junior stood at the plate with Al Senior on the pitcher's mound, and the two faced each other with muscles tensed. Finally, Al Senior lifted his arm and swung the ball high over his head—twice around the world. With a flourish, the shot was released. It streaked across the field like a bullet on the rip.

A loud crack rent the air, and the missile whizzed into the outfield. Michael Ames ran toward it, bounding upward with his mitt held high—but the ball sailed past his reaching arm and fell into the tall grass beyond range. Young Al trotted around the bases toward home plate. But the game was at an end.

Clang, clang, clang! The fire bell echoed across the land, announcing the end of fun and games. Faces grew tense and muscles bulged. Neighbors scanned the countryside for danger —and there it was, smoke billowing in the direction of Camp 8. The event was over. Everyone ran for their wagons.

The world was thrown into turmoil.

Adrenaline shot up Clive's spine as he leapt aboard the family's carriage. "C'mon, Blackie!" he shouted. "C'mon, Gunnar!" He flicked the reins, and the transport rolled over the ground at top speed. It raced past Hitchcock's Store, rounded the bend by Hans Kubeck's blacksmith shop, and flew by the Weavers' house. Then it turned up the lane toward Camp 8, and Clive saw the flames. They billowed along the tree line, sending sparks flying unrestrained into the air. "Whoa," Clive called, and the carriage came to a stop near the cook shanty. He threw the reins over the dash, hopped onto the ground, and released the horses. "You women secure things around here," he shouted. "And get Faith Ann to dousing sparks in the haystack. If that hay catches fire, it'll take the whole place."

"C'mon, Adam!" he called, and the two men ran toward the tool shed. Arriving at the building, Clive opened the latch, flung the door wide, and reached for the broadest shovel in the place.

Adam grabbed a nearby spade, and they exited the building on the run.

Outside, Tom Morse's wagon clattered up the lane and into the yard. It came to a stop near the barn, and a team of men vaulted onto the ground, carrying weapons of war. There were axes, blankets, shovels—whatever item might be used to beat at the blaze.

"C'mon!" Tom shouted and the crew hurtled en masse toward the conflagration, skirting the stumps that dotted the ground. Dry brush lay in piles here and there—left years ago by lumbermen who had harvested the giant pines. Now that tinder would provide abundant fuel for the holocaust that raged in Clive's back yard.

Soon the firefighters arrived at the site of the blaze to find the undergrowth erupting everywhere they looked. They confronted the menace, slamming at it with all their strength. Sweat rolled down their cheeks, and skin chafed in the scorching heat, but with each strike a small part of the inferno was extinguished. Clive lifted his wide-edged shovel and brought it down hard on the flames. Adam beat at the blaze with his spade, and Tom Morse dumped dirt onto the flares with his shovel.

At Camp 8, Katherine hung a bucket on the pump and hauled down on the handle. Water splashed into the pail, rising steadily until the container was full. Then she turned to her daughter. "Come on, Faith Ann," she said. "You have work to do." She led the little girl around the tool shed to the barn, explaining the gravity of the task that was about to be assigned. "Sweetheart, you have a very important job," she said. "You just may be the one who saves the farm."

As they neared the haystack, a spark dropped into the dried grass. It crackled in its resting place and began to glow. In an instant, Katherine filled the dipper, ran to the glowing coal, and soaked the ember. "There," she said, looking down at Faith Ann. "That's what you're supposed to do. Every time a spark falls into the hay, you are to douse it."

"I can do it," the little girl said—but her troubled eyes and trembling lips told a much-less-assured story.

Katherine bent and put her arms around the girl's shoulder. "Hannah and I will be right here," she said. "If you need help, just holler, and we'll come running."

Immediately, a spark fell into the hay, and Faith Ann pulled away from her mother. She grabbed the dipper, filled it with water and soaked the incendiary into oblivion. Then she turned to Katherine with a grin. "See, I can do it." Her face flushed with newfound courage.

"I see that," Katherine said. She hugged her little girl and returned to her job of securing the farm. As she came around the corner of the tool shed, she found Hannah with Verna Weaver and Aunt Mae, soaking everything within sight and extinguishing any sparks that fell into the grass.

Nearby Bobby Weaver stood watching, wide-eyed and awestruck.

"Faith Ann is out behind the barn," Katherine said. "She's keeping the fire from burning the haystack. You want to go out there and help?"

The boy nodded, and Katherine led him around the tool shed, where he took the tin cup she offered and went to work, helping the not-so-little girl to protect her family's property, and perhaps even the entire community.

All afternoon the community worked. They pounded the flames. They doused the sparks. They cleared the fire lane. Then about six o'clock, the women prepared a meal, and the men came in shifts for soup, sandwiches, and water. They grabbed a bite to eat and returned to their job in the field.

Finally, about seven thirty, the wind shifted. The blaze raced north, and the men were able to quench the last of the flames in the backyard. Tears of relief trickled down soot-blackened faces, and women wept openly. The countryside was charred into a gray haze, and the forest was a maze of blackened stubs—but the community was saved. They turned and made their way back to their farms.

Exhausted, Clive brushed his arm across his brow to clear the sweat that trickled into his eyes.

CHAPTER 12

SETH STROLLED THROUGH the forest, enjoying the solitude that personified the deep woods. He admired the giant pines that had stood for hundreds of years, growing ever taller as the world passed from one generation to another. He looked up at their crowns and noticed the flutter of leaves in the breeze as it passed by on its way to forever.

Looking down at the earth, he noticed a deep rut that straggled through the soil. It was there that yesterday's harvest had been hauled to the decking grounds. While one end of the logs dangled from the chain on the big wheels, the other end had dragged on the ground, leaving this trail in the dirt.

As Seth stood contemplating his surroundings an eerie silence overspread his consciousness. There were no birds in the trees and no squirrels skittering over the forest floor. He waited, trying to calm the sense of imminent peril that festered in his gut.

Then the world exploded. A thunderous roar reverberated in the treetops. The blaze crackled and hissed as beads of sap kindled and burst into flame. Seth was caught, surrounded by a triangle of death. The young man raced in the only direction that was not engulfed in the conflagration. The river, where was the river?

His only goal was escape. He had to find cover . . . a cave . . . a hole in the ground . . . something. He peered through the blistering heat, unable to focus because of the smoke. Then he saw it, a fallen tree with roots rising from the cavern where it had stood. He threw himself at its stock, burrowing deep into the space under its bole, hoping against hope that the fire wouldn't suck the breath from his lungs.

As he huddled in the darkness, a soft moan resonated in the space below. A tuft of fur touched his arm, revealing a little bear cub nestled in the cavern beneath him. The animal moved, burrowing deeper into the depths of the cavern—and there, revealed in a gasp of fresh air, was a tiny passage into the interior. "Hey fella," Seth murmured. "I guess we're in this together . . . and at least we have air to breathe." He drew close to the baby and it snuggled against his side. The two huddled together, man and beast seeking comfort in distress.

Seth took a shallow breath and waited, noticing the aroma of musk even as he sweltered in the unfathomable heat. Then the world grew hazy. His mind whirled and blackness descended. He lay motionless.

Hannah's heart ached with sorrow as she walked down a two track road toward the old red barn. She kicked at a stone, and it rolled into the dirt, resting in the charred remains of a once green and growing field. She peered across the countryside at what had once been verdant trees but that now bore stubby arms that were shrouded in soot. Looking up, she missed her footing and nearly stumbled over an animal's charred remains. A porcupine had been unable to escape the flames. He lay lifeless in the dirt. Hannah sighed and turned up the lane toward the old red barn where she had stashed Seth's supplies after he left.

Then she stopped. She gulped, staring at the world with saucer eyes as the reality of what lay before her gripped her mind. Mounds of rubble lay across the land, charred and ruined. A heap of ashes marked the site where the building had stood. One particular pile of debris caught Hannah's attention, unrecognizable except for the iron pot—black and wasted and lying on its side. The young woman stood transfixed, an empty ache gnawed at her soul.

She thought of her neighbors, beating back the flames with shovels and blankets and old rugs, keeping the fire from eating her home. She thought of Faith Ann and Bobby, dousing the sparks that flew into the hay . . . and she thought of Seth. Where was her brother? Had he found shelter? Was he safe, or was he dead like the porcupine that lay along the road? What terrible thing had he done that prevented his coming home?

Seth crawled out of the cave and flexed his shoulders. A sharp pain revealed a burn across his back, and he winced. Then he looked around for something familiar that would take him to the Farleys' camp.

As the young man pondered, he felt a soft caress against his leg and looked down to find his friend, the little bear, snuggling against him. "Well, hello there," he said. "I guess we made it together. I think that makes us buddies." The cub returned the sentiment with eyes that reached out for comfort in a lost world. "I'm sorry, little guy," the young man crooned. "If it's direction you want, I'm not much help."

Then he reached down to pat the animal. "Roots," he said. "I think I'll call you Roots." Roots turned, took several steps and looked back at Seth with hurting eyes.

"Okay, little guy," he said. "We can stick together for a while anyway." Seth stood erect, scrutinizing his surroundings. Finally, he looked up at the sky and started moving toward the sun in search of something to guide his way.

As the two friends walked through the bleak terrain, each step churned the black ash underfoot. Bits of soot clung to their bodies like gnats. Seth rubbed at the sooty particles, and black streaks appeared on his arms. He wondered if his face were as besmirched as his limbs.

Then he noticed an open area ahead. He stumbled toward it, and in his haste he tripped over a rock. His body flew headlong into the grime. "Grouch!" he groused at his own ineptness. He rose, brushed himself off and clamored forward toward the opening—and there to his relief lay a long jagged rut creasing the ground. It was the skid road where horses hauled logs to the decking grounds. It was a path to life itself. "C'mon, fella," he whooped. "We got 'er made."

Clive stood with Katherine, overlooking the desolation that was their farm. Crops that hadn't been seared by fire had been trampled by men. Nothing was left but the buildings—no wheat, no corn, no hay—and no way to provide for the long winter months ahead.

"You know," Katherine said, "it could be worse. We still have each other, our family is safe, and our home is intact. We'll be okay."

But Clive's fears were not assuaged. His family needed money, and with a new baby on the way, the need was even greater. He turned and moved toward the cook shanty with Katherine by his side. They walked along hand in hand until they noticed Jasper coming up the lane in his carriage. Clive had spent many winters working with Jasper in the lumber camps.

"Hey, Jasper," Clive called as the man came near. "What's up?"

Jasper climbed down from his transport and reached out his hand. "Just wondering how you're doing," he said.

Clive pasted a smile on his face. "Things are a bit tough as you might expect, but we'll make it."

Jasper shook his head in commiseration. "That fire was a really rotten affair," he said.

"Well, we'll get by," Clive responded. "The first year we were here, we harvested hay by the railroad tracks and ate pancakes with syrup made of boiled maple bark. We made it, and we can do it again."

"Well, I'm here to tell you that you don't have to struggle through all that another time."

Clive's eyes widened and his brow raised. He brushed his hand over his dark curly hair and gazed at the man. "So what have you got up your sleeve?"

"Let's go inside where we can talk."

Clive turned and led the way toward the cook shanty, wondering what the man was thinking.

"Coffee?" Katherine said as they entered. "Don't mind if I do," Jasper responded.

Clive and Jasper took their places at the table, while Katherine poured. "Seriously, Clive, I have an answer to the problems that were caused by the fire," Jasper said.

"Yes?"

Jasper took a sip from his cup and set it on the table. "Waterhouse is looking for a walker to oversee the camps." He looked from Clive to Katherine and back to Clive

An unbidden surge quivered in Clive's chest. His heart whisked away to the forest with its chattering birds and rushing rivers and swirling snow banks. Then he jerked himself back to reality. He had a family, and he had promised he'd never leave them alone.

Jasper's eyes grew intense. "Waterhouse really needs a good walker, and they'd hire you in a minute."

Clive tried to swallow the lump that dominated his throat. "I'd be happy to oblige," he said, "but I just can't go off and leave my family all winter." He glanced at his wife but saw no sign that would reveal her feelings. "Besides, Katherine's in the family way, and I don't want to miss this baby's birth."

"Well, think about it," Jasper said. He rose to his feet and moved toward the door. "It'd be a real help to you as you ride out the loss that fire has created."

Clive and Katherine followed the man outside, where they stood bidding him goodbye.

"It's a good job," Jasper said, "and it'd make a big difference for you and your family." The man settled himself in his carriage and reached for the reins. "Think about it," he called. He flicked the leads and left.

Later Clive stood in the tool shed mending harnesses and considering the offer. What was best—to go or not to go? One winter spent in his old habitat could really help his family financially. He reached for a rivet, placed it over the joint in the strap, and gave it a tap. He just didn't know what to do. He finished fixing the harness, hung it over a nail, and headed toward the cook shanty.

Inside Katherine came near and took a seat beside him on the settee. "Clive," she whispered, "we need to talk about Jasper's offer."

"You're right, of course," he responded. "I've been thinking about it all day."

Katherine rested her hand on his knee. "I think you should go," she said.

Clive's stomach contracted into a knot. "But, what about you and the baby? How can I go and leave you alone to deliver my baby again?"

"Maybe you could get some time off when the baby's due," Katherine replied. "Jasper said they really want you, and they might be willing to make some concessions."

"But you'd be alone," Clive responded.

"Granny Weemes is about two miles down the road," Katherine went on. "And Hannah and Adam are both here. Either of them could go for her at a moment's notice. She could be with me in minutes."

"You sound like you want to get rid of me."

Katherine's face twisted into a frown. "Clive, you know better."

"Well?"

"It's all about the money; we need the money."

A bleak, wintry storm crept over Clive's heart. He knew she was right. He had to go, but he didn't have to like it.

"Those camp bosses know what they're doing," she said. "They can handle things for a few days without you, when this baby is due." Without another word Clive's beautiful wife rose and pulled the pins from her hair, allowing it to fall like sunshine around her shoulders. "It's not that I want you to go; you know that. It's just that the money you'd make for doing what you love would really come in handy." She reached out to him. "Now, let's go to bed."

Clive's heart swelled with emotion for this woman he'd loved since they were teenagers. With her encouragement, he could do anything. Maybe she was right. He'd check the possibilities.

Hannah sat on her bed, considering the future. Verena Spencer had announced her engagement, and that meant the town would have no teacher. They'd have to close the school.

On the other hand, the Isaman family needed money to rebound after the fire. If Hannah went to County Normal in Boyne City for six weeks, she could take the position. It was a good job, and it would be a big help to her family.

Hannah was sure it was the right thing to do.

CHAPTER 13

OPTIMISM AND FEAR battled for Seth's psyche as he made his way toward the Farley camp with Roots at his side. Had the Farleys survived? They were experienced woodsmen. They would have known what to do. Surely they were okay.

Before long the two friends came to a dirt road that led to the site. "C'mon, fella," Seth said. "We're almost there." He patted his friend's side and took off on the run.

As they broke into the clearing, Seth's heart broke. The place was unlivable. Burned rafters and studs pointed skyward through what had been the roof of the cook shanty. A pile of rubble marked the place where the barn had stood, and there was no sign of the Farleys. Roots brushed against him as if in consolation.

As the young man wandered among the ruins, he noticed the charred remains of a whittled out sailboat. He kicked it aside and moved toward the ruined cook shanty. Tears threatened to escape his eyes.

Suddenly a voice rang out. "Jeb!" The Farley men emerged from behind a pile of debris.

A tide of joy surged in Seth's chest. "Max!" he yelled. "Ike!" In a flash, the men were face to face, all talking at once.

"What happened to you?"

"Is everybody safe?"

"You scared us to death."

"Where's Eric and Dean and Harriet?"

"How'd you escape the fire?"

"Were you able to save the horses?"

When at last the excitement slowed to a reasonable pace, Seth told his story. He told of the raging fire. He told of finding the fallen tree and burying himself in its cavity. He told of Roots and the friendship he'd formed with the little guy. Then he looked around. Where was Roots? Where was his friend?

With trembling heart, Seth looked around the site. He looked at the burned out buildings. He looked at the river. He looked at the charred ground. Then he looked along the tree line and there, waiting in the underbrush, frightened, alone and lonely, stood his comrade. Seth's heart broke.

"Well, at least you're okay." Ike broke into Seth's thoughts, delivering a congratulatory slap to his back. Pain shot through the young man's body. He winced and pulled away.

"Are you all right?" Ike stepped back.

"I'm okay," Seth said. "But I got a little burn back there."

"Well let's go get that taken care of right now," Max said. The three men made their way to the river's edge, climbed onto a raft that waited there, and poled it across the flow toward a makeshift encampment. As they went, Seth looked back to see Roots. The bear was running along the river's edge, trilling and chipping. The young man's heart went out to a little fellow who was alone and desolate in a forlorn world.

Finally, the Farleys reached the shore, and Eric and Dean waded into the shallows. "Jeb!" they called out. "Where were you? We were scared for you."

"I'm okay!" Seth responded. "I'll tell you all about it in a minute." The group made their way to the encampment and everyone gathered around as Seth retold his story.

"Folks, I'd like you to meet Fireproof Farley," Max said as the

71

account ended. Without thinking, he slapped Seth on the back.

Seth drew back in pain. "Well, not entirely fireproof," he said, "but certainly glad to be here with you folks."

Harriet's eyes grew wide. "You're hurt. C'mon, we better get you fixed up."

Seth followed his surrogate mother to the camp bench, where she pulled off his shirt. She covered his back with a bread-and-milk poultice and declared him remedied. "There," she said. "That should draw out the pain."

Katherine lay beside her husband with her mind in turmoil. She hated the thought of the long lonely nights and solitary days that she knew were coming. She didn't look forward to spending night after night alone in an empty bed, and she certainly didn't need the agitation that would be present in dealing with Hannah's attitude toward Adam Beste . . . but the family needed money, and she knew Clive had warm feelings for the woods. For that reason, she had encouraged her husband to leave the farm and take a job as walker for Waterhouse Lumber Company.

Reaching across the bed, she touched the man she loved. He let out a long heavy sigh and lay still as a stone. Was he awake and suffering with the decision he must make?

Katherine's lips drew into a sad smile. She knew the pain her husband was feeling, and she ached for him. She lay by his side, waiting for morning.

Hannah sat on the ground near Torrie's Spring, holding a letter from her grandma. She opened it, reading through her tears.

Dear Hannah,
 How are you? We're still looking for Seth. We're so worried

about him. He was here one day and the next he was gone. We filled out a report for Sheriff Duncan, but we still haven't heard a thing. Let us know if you learn anything.
Grandma and Grandpa McLean

Without warning weeks of pain and worry broke loose, and Hannah exploded into tears. *Seth, where are you? What have you done?* She covered her eyes with her hands, sobbing bitterly. *Everyone's worried about you, and I can't keep your secret much longer.* Her wailing rent the air as pain flowed from her aching body. Then she released it all and sat weeping into her palms.

In time she opened her eyes to see Adam Beste standing over her. Instantly her frustration and anger broke loose. She leapt to her feet, screaming in his face. "What are you doing here? Why do you keep following me around? First, you impose yourself into Sam Hitchcock's store and hang over me like a wet towel. Then you move onto our property, where you're always in my face. Who are you anyway, and why don't you just go away and find someone else to annoy?"

Adam stood silent; his face registered nothing.

"Well?"

"Hannah, I don't mean to bother you. I'm just as worried about Seth as you are."

Hannah fell back, eyes wide with astonishment. What was this interloper talking about?

"Please don't push me away any longer, Hannah. Let's work together. I can help you."

"How can you help me? You don't know me, and you don't know anything about me. You're just an unwanted intruder who doesn't belong here, messing around in my business."

"I came here looking for Seth."

Hannah's eyes grew into saucers. "What are you talking about?"

"Seth and I were out shooting crows together, and there was an accident. I blacked out and the next thing I knew I was at the doctor's office . . . and Seth was gone."

Hannah gasped; her world turned gray and her head reeled. "And you just want to help Seth?"

"That's right, I can't let him go on running forever. C'mon, sit here on this log, and I'll tell you all I know."

Hannah and Adam sat near the spring for many long minutes, going over the events that had brought them together. "So now we can tell everyone that Seth was here," Adam said at last.

Hannah's stomach clenched. "No, I can't do that. I promised."

"But things are different now. If we all work together, we can save your brother from a life of running from himself."

Hannah sat silent. Her world had just tipped upside down.

"We can tell them what we know after Clive comes in from the fields tonight."

"Wait," Hannah said. "I need some time. It's all so new."

"Okay," Adam said, "but we need to tell them soon. The longer we wait, the farther away Seth may have run."

Katherine stood in the kitchen peeling potatoes when Faith Ann's voice pierced the air. "Mama!" the little girl yelled. The scream was enough to frighten the most fearless warrior, and Katherine was no exception. She tossed the potato into the water and ran to her daughter's defense.

She stepped outside and stopped short. The little girl's new puppy stood in the water dish with feet spinning like a top. Water splashed everywhere, and Faith Ann stood, dripping wet—soaked to the gills. Katherine stood on the porch, caught in a peal of unrestrained laughter.

"It's not funny," the little girl blurted.

Katherine ran to her child. "Sassy, get out of there," she commanded. She shoved the dog aside, dumped water from the dish, and pulled her little girl into a cold and wet hug. Thus both mother and daughter felt the chill of the cold water.

"You'll be all right, sweetheart," Katherine said. She ushered her daughter inside and led her to the room behind the wall. She helped the girl out of her wet clothing, handed her a towel, and provided a clean set of underwear and other garments. "Now," she said, "you get dressed while I take care of this wet stuff."

Katherine carried the soaked clothing outside and draped it over the line. When she looked up she saw Hannah and Adam, walking up the lane together. They seemed almost friendly. She shook her head in dismay. Katherine would never understand that girl.

CHAPTER 14

ADAM SAT IN the tool shed at Camp 8, scanning the *County Farmer* magazine without reading a word. Hannah had promised to tell the family about Seth's appearance in Hitchcock, and tonight was the night. Then the family could work together to find Seth.

Finally the door opened, and Faith Ann entered. "Supper's ready," she called.

"Okay, I'm coming." Adam tossed the magazine aside and followed the girl across the yard. He entered the cook shanty to find a platter of roast beef waiting on the table with mashed potatoes and gravy. "Something sure smells good in here," he said.

"Adam's here," Hannah called. "Let's eat." With that, the family took their places for the meal, and Clive said grace. "Thank you, Lord, for this food," he prayed, "and for the joy of being a family and working together as one for the good of all."

Adam's heart skipped a beat. It was almost as if Clive had some perception of the revelation that was about to come.

But Hannah sat without a word.

After the meal Hannah went to the kitchen with Katherine and Faith Ann, having said nothing, and Adam fidgeted. Why didn't she just do it and get it over with?

"How about a game of checkers?" Clive suggested.

"You're on," Adam responded. Although his mind was aflutter and he could lose the game, it would be better than just sitting there.

Clive reached into the buffet drawer for the board and laid it out on the table. He chose the black checkers for himself and shoved the red ones across to Adam.

Adam placed his game pieces on the board and sat mulling over the activity in the kitchen. What was Hannah doing? Why didn't she just do what had to be done?

"Adam," Clive said. "It's your turn."

"Oh." Adam paused, scanning the red and black squares for a move that would advance his cause. He tapped the table with his fingertips and bobbled his foot on the floor. Then he moved a man one space forward. He didn't know what he might gain by the move, but the game proceeded.

Finally, Hannah finished her work in the kitchen. She appeared in the doorway, looked around, and moved near the table. She took a seat and sat silently watching the game.

Adam stared at the discs on the table with his mind flitting from Hannah to the game and back to Hannah. Why didn't she just do it and get it done? *C'mon, girl, I'll help you.* It was Adam's turn and he forced his attention to the game. He jumped his red king backward with a flourish, taking out two of Clive's black men and reducing his host's players to five.

At that point Clive's face lit up, radiating with the glow of victory. He jumped the last of Adam's men and removed them from the board. The game was over, and Clive had won. The checkers were cleared away, and the family paused in transition.

Then Hannah made her move. She cleared her throat and reached out to her stepmother. "Katherine," she said, "come over here and sit with us, will you? There's something I need to tell you."

Katherine's brow furrowed as she moved away from the buffet and took a seat at the table.

"You remember last spring," Hannah said, "when I kept wandering off for long periods of time, and then not wanting to talk about it when I returned?" She expelled the words quickly, as if to get beyond the unpleasant moment.

"Yes," Katherine responded, "but it passed, and I decided you just needed a little time to yourself."

"I told you I was down by the spring," Hannah said, "but that wasn't true. Seth was hiding in the chasm by Little Birch Lake, and I was going there to be with him." Tears beaded behind her eyes.

"What?" Katherine glared at Hannah. "Seth was here and you didn't bring him home?" She scoured the girl's face. "I can't believe you did that."

Sudden comprehension filled Clive's countenance. "So that's who was staying out there in that hut," he said.

Then Katherine's eyes grew moist. "Hannah, how could you do this to us—and what about your grandparents? They've been worried sick about Seth."

Tears rolled down Hannah's cheeks. "He wouldn't come home with me," she responded. "I kept asking, but he wouldn't. He made me promise not to even tell you he was around."

"So where is he now?"

"When Wolf was killed he said he had to get away before someone came looking for the dead fox."

At that point Adam broke into the discussion. "Seth was my best friend back in Bounding," he said. "Then one day we were out shooting crows together, and somehow I ended up at the doctor's office with blood all over me. Seth was gone, and I have no idea where he went."

"So, he shot you and then ran away without knowing how bad it was." Clive sat still, meditative and concerned.

"That's right . . . and I've got to find him. Who knows what he's thinking or what he'll do to himself?"

Clive brushed his hands through his hair. "Well," he said, "I'm going to the camps. As walker for Waterhouse, I'll get around. Maybe someone will have word of him."

"That's one reason it's so important for you to know about this," Adam responded. "If we work together, we have a better chance to find him."

Later that night Adam lay on his bunk considering the evening's events. Maybe he should go to the camps himself. Clive had never seen Seth. The young man could walk right past Clive and never be noticed. Tomorrow Adam would talk to Sam about the possibility of getting time off.

Hannah sat in the teacher education class in Boyne City. A tall, skinny woman about fifty years old stood in front of the room with twelve sets of eyes watching her every move. The woman brushed her hand over her yellowish gray hair that had been pulled back into a bun. She picked up a piece of chalk and turned to the blackboard, *Mrs. Tory,* she wrote. Then she turned.

"Ladies," she said, "I'm Mrs. Tory. You came here to learn to be teachers, and I mean to give you the best training that I can. Work hard, and you'll leave here in six weeks, ready to step into the classroom."

Hannah adjusted her notebook and prepared to learn all she could over the next six weeks.

CHAPTER 15

KATHERINE WATCHED AS Clive walked down the lane and out of her reach. Soon he'd meet Jasper, and the two men would head into the woods. Tears welled in her eyes, trickling slowly down her cheeks. She remembered a time, not long ago, when her first husband had left for the camps. Then, before the winter was finished, he was gone, killed by a swinging limb. Now a second husband had left her behind on his way into the deep and dangerous woods.

At the end of the lane Clive turned. He looked back and lifted his hand to his lips, flinging it outward and tossing her a kiss. Then he disappeared around the bend onto Boyne City Road. "Goodbye, my love," she whispered. "Goodbye."

She turned and entered her cook shanty home, and the memory of Frank's death came crashing down—the emptiness, the isolation, the responsibility. "Why, God?" she murmured. "Why must I be left behind again?"

Outside Sassy began to bark, and Katherine knew that Faith Ann was coming up the lane from school. She must leave off feeling sorry for herself and be a mother to her child. Maybe they'd take a little walk in the woods and visit Torrie's Spring where the water always flowed clean and constant and pure. She needed to get away, to take a little break from the pressure of the day.

Clive entered the office at Camp DuBois and tossed his backpack onto the bunk. "Well, here we are," he said. "How's it going?"

"Fine, so far," Luc DuBois responded. "Let's go over and meet the crew."

Clive and Luc crossed the road to the cook shanty, where they found tote master, Gabby Helms, regaling everyone who would listen. "This little kid, he had steel in his bones," the old man said. "He didn't back down fer nothin' er nobody. He just looked up at big old Mike Bellows and hollered, 'I don't think you can do it.'"

Clive grinned at Luc and took a seat as Emma McLean poured coffee. Gabby could always be counted on to entertain the crowd with an outrageous tale of the woods.

"Well, ol' Mike, he didn't take to no such talk," Gabby went on. The man peered into each face, amplifying the tension in the room. "Ole Mike's cheeks got red and puffy, and his eyes glared 'til the whole room blazed with their light. He growled so loud, the sound thundered across the land for three days. Then he tore across the room at that little kid."

Gabby paused for several long seconds. "But the kid was too quick fer old Mike. He jumped outta the way, and that mean old fella went a-flyin' straight into the stove like a bullet out o' hell. He smashed his ugly mug on that redhot heater and burned it to a flaming blister."

Gabby slammed his fist into his hand. "And I'll bet old Mike's face is still a burnin' today."

The room grew silent. The account was finished.

Just then Emma appeared with a dish of molasses cookies and a fresh pot of coffee. "C'mon, boys," she sang. "We got morning mud 'n blackstrap biscuits." Not a man in the room turned down the proffered treat.

The next morning Clive, Luc, and Jasper made their way into the deep woods to plan the layout for the camp. "We'll run the hauling road through here," Luc said. "It'll go around that swale, past the clump of underbrush, and straight to the decking grounds at the river. Then the branch roads can come in on either side."

Both Clive and Jasper nodded their agreement, and the work was finished for the day. "Let's get on back to camp for supper," Luc said.

It was Saturday, and Adam sat at the police station in Boyne City, waiting to see Sheriff Payne. He tapped his fingers on the arm of the chair as he rehearsed his presentation. *Sheriff, I have great information for you.* Or maybe he should be a little more laid back. *Sheriff,* he might say, *I'm just checking to see how things are going.*

At last the door to the inner office opened and the clerk appeared. "Mr. Payne will see you now," he said. He took a seat behind the desk and reached for a stack of papers.

"Well, young man," Sheriff Payne said as Adam stepped into the office, "I see you're back."

"Yes, and I have good news."

The sheriff didn't seem to grasp the hopeful tone in Adam's voice. "I'm sorry, but nothing's changed. We haven't seen hide nor hair of your friend."

Adam seated himself near the desk and looked into the law man's face. "But I've learned something new, something that might help."

Sheriff Payne sighed and remained indifferent. "Young man, I've tried to tell you; there is really very little hope of finding your friend. He can hide out there until he's good and ready to be found."

"But I have some new information." Adam repeated the assertion for the third time. "I talked to his sister, and she said he'd been to their place and he was coming this way."

The sheriff raised his right eyebrow and looked across at Adam with renewed curiosity. "So, just exactly where did this girl say your young man had been, and where was he going?"

"Well, I don't know exactly."

Sheriff Payne fell back in his chair. "So the truth is you don't really have anything new to report."

"Well, just that he was here, and we know he came this way." Without warning a man burst into the office, bristling with tension. The veins in his neck pulsed and his fists balled. "Don," he said, "Big Mackie is in town. He's over in Connors Alley, and he's creating all kinds of havoc." The man leaned over the sheriff's desk, totally ignoring Adam's presence.

The sheriff's face grew red, and his brow furrowed. "I guess that's all, young man," he said. He didn't even look at Adam. He just nodded toward the door in dismissal.

Adam exited the building feeling ignored and let down. He knew the chances of change were miniscule, yet it hurt to the soles of his feet to hear Sheriff Payne sing the same old song time after time. The young man turned and headed down Main Street toward the Lewis home and Hannah. At least he'd get some time with his new friend while he was in town.

As he walked, he noticed the trees along Main Street, blossoming with brilliant hues of red and yellow and orange. It was a beautiful time of year that would have brought peace and tranquility, were it not for the pain in his soul.

Finally, he arrived at the Lewis home and knocked on the door.

"Adam!" Hannah exclaimed as she found him standing there. "What're you doing here?"

"Just stopped by to say hello and let you know about my talk with the sheriff," Adam said.

"Well, come in and meet Mrs. Lewis." Hannah led the young man into the sitting room, where an old lady sat in her rocking chair with eyes closed, resting. "Mrs. Lewis, I'd like you to meet my friend, Adam Beste," Hannah said. The old lady opened her eyes and peered over her glasses. "It's nice to meet you, Adam," she said.

Adam nodded. "It's nice to meet you too, Mrs. Lewis."

The old lady's eyes wavered and she returned to dreamland. Hannah motioned for Adam to follow her to the kitchen.

"So what happened?" Hannah said as she entered the room. "Did Sheriff Payne seem any more interested?"

"Not a bit," Adam responded. "In fact, some guy burst in the office and interrupted our talk. The sheriff just sent me packing."

Hannah motioned toward a chair and Adam took a seat. Then he launched into the story of his visit with Sheriff Payne, the intrusion of the deputy, and his own disappointment.

"Well, I'm not surprised." Hannah flicked a lock of hair back off her face. "He's no different than he's always been."

"So how are things with you?" Adam said.

"Not bad." Hannah responded. "Sometimes I get frustrated when my duties here conflict with my studies. But the Lewises are good people, and this way I get my room and board for free."

"Well, you'll be done with your classes soon, and then you can come home."

"I'll come home sooner than you think," Hannah said. "I get a week off for Thanksgiving."

Adam's heart surged. "Great! I guess Thanksgiving dinner will be at your place, so you'll be right at home."

The afternoon passed with laughing and talking and sharing. Then in time, Adam noticed the clock. "Well, I guess I better be going," he said. "I need to check in at the hotel so I'll be ready to leave first thing in the morning."

Hannah walked Adam to the door. "Well, I'm glad you came," she said, as they stood saying goodbye. "It made my day."

Adam looked deep into the young woman's eyes, wondering if he dared to give her a hug—no, he guessed he better not. He left and made his way to the hotel.

CHAPTER 16

CLIVE STEPPED INTO the clearing at the Farley camp and looked about. The entire site was covered with ashes. The barn stood like a ghost of the past, and the cook shanty trembled on its moorings. Moving closer, he saw a temporary camp across the river and called out. "Hello over there, is anyone around?"

Two young boys ran to the water's edge, waving and shouting. "Hi there, Mister. We're the Farleys. Who are you?"

"I'm the Waterhouse walker," Clive yelled. "Is Max Farley around?"

The boys took off on the run, leaving Clive to contemplate his mission. He needed to get across that river where he could talk to Max Farley about an offer from Waterhouse. He stood watching and waiting.

Soon the boys returned, accompanied by a young man who appeared to be an older brother. They pulled a raft from among the reeds and the elder sibling climbed aboard, poling his way across the water.

"I'm Wade Farley," the young man said as he came near. "Max Farley is my pa. Is there anything I can help you with?"

"I don't think so," Clive responded. "I need to talk to the boss."

"Well, hop aboard. He's cutting firewood with my pa and Jeb, but they'll be home soon, and you can see him then." Clive stepped onto the transport and the young man shoved off.

As the craft skidded ashore on the other side of the river, the boys came running. "I'm Eric," one of them sang. "And I'm Dean," the other added. "Our ma is over there."

The four males walked toward the campfire to find two women standing over a cooking pot. "I'm Harriet Farley," said the older woman as they approached. "My father-in-law runs this camp. What can I do for you?"

"I've got an offer from Waterhouse about a tract they want to get harvested, and I need to talk to the man in charge."

"Well, Pa'll be home soon and you can talk to him."

Clive nodded and took a seat by the table, making small talk to fill time. "So how are things?" he said.

"Fine, fine." Harriet responded. "That fire did us real damage, but we're making it."

The afternoon passed, and in time three men came walking into camp. "I'm Max Farley," the older man said as they met, "This is my son Ike and this is Jeb."

"It's nice to meet you folks," Clive responded. "Harriet says you got hit pretty hard by the fire that ran through here a bit ago."

"Yes," Max said, "but at least we saved the animals. We got a lot of cleaning up to do but we'll make it."

"Well, maybe I can help," Clive responded. There was no answer, so he went on. "Waterhouse has acquired a little tract of land from B&W Railroad. It's just out of reach for the DuBois camp and they need a jobber to harvest the trees. If you choose to take the job, DuBois will build the roads and haul supplies. All you have to do is cut the timber and get it to the supply route."

Clive pulled a map out of his backpack and laid it out for viewing. "This is the territory we're offering. Terms will be as usual—a hundred dollars for a thousand feet of timber—and we'll bring in a spur for transportation."

Max tucked his thumbs under his suspenders. "It sounds reasonable," he said. "Let me think it over. We'll let you know."

With that Clive went on his way. He had a dozen camps to oversee, and he wanted to get the planning finished so he could be home for the new year and his baby's birth.

It was Thanksgiving Day, and Katherine was hosting the event for the very first time. Yesterday she had killed the rooster and let the blood run out. Then when he was ready, she brought him inside, drenched him in boiling water to loosen the feathers, and plucked him clean. Finally that mean old fowl had met his end, and Katherine wasn't sorry. She was sick and tired of his nasty disposition, trying to run her off every time she came near the henhouse.

This morning Katherine had filled the bird with sausage stuffing, placed the giblets in the neck cavity, and put the bird in the oven. Then she turned her attention to the rag-bag pudding. Stirring the raisins and suet together with other sweetmeats, she pressed the mixture into a sack and put it to steam. In about three hours, it would become a delicious side dish.

Katherine was a bit jittery today because Aunt Mae had always been in charge of everything. It was a little daunting to think about having the woman looking over her shoulder all day. But Aunt Mae was a good person. She had always been kind to Katherine, and Katherine wouldn't hurt her feelings for the world. She squared her shoulders and moved forward with the planning.

A rustle in the other room caught Katherine's attention and she turned. "Good morning, Hannah," she said. "Did you sleep well?"

"Good morning," Hannah responded. "Slept like a baby in my own bed with Faith Ann to cuddle up to." Coming near the range, the young woman held her hands over the firepot, rubbing them together for warmth. Then she stepped back. "Okay, what can I do to help?"

Katherine nodded toward the dishpan sitting on the cabinet. "Go down to the root cellar, if you will, and get some potatoes for dinner."

"Sure thing." Hannah reached for the container and headed outside.

"And get some carrots and a few onions while you're down there," Katherine called.

Soon Hannah returned to the kitchen with the pan full of potatoes. She took an apron from the pantry, slipped it over her head, and set about peeling the tubers for dinner. It was then that a soft rap announced the arrival of company.

"Hi, everyone," Adam called. He pulled open the door and stepped inside. "Is there anything I can do to help?"

"Adam, c'mon in," Hannah sang. The girl put on her most compelling smile.

Katherine shook her head in wonderment. Things certainly had changed between those two since the news of Seth's appearance came to light. She put the vegetables in the warming oven and picked up a paring knife.

Soon the clip-clop of horses' hooves resounded on the driveway, announcing the arrival of their guests. Aunt Mae and Uncle Ned had arrived, with the Weavers close behind. Both carriages came to a stop near the cook shanty. Then the world flew into a frenzy. There were smiles, hugs, and greetings, with everyone talking at once.

"How you doing?"

"What can I do to help?"

"Come on in and make yourselves comfortable."

"Have you seen that new . . ."

"I brought along a . . ."

Finally everyone made their way inside where Aunt Mae took control. "Put the pies on the pantry shelf," she commanded.

"And Verna, the sweet potatoes and creamed spinach should go in the warming oven. Al, close the door, will you?"

Katherine smiled a bit ruefully. Nothing had changed. Aunt Mae still ruled the roost.

"Now, then," Aunt Mae turned her attention to the furniture arrangement, "you men go out to the barn and get some stuff to build a bench. We can pull the sideboard up to the dining table to make extra space, and Hannah, why don't you get a couple of sheets to use for tablecloths?" Everyone performed his or her task in accordance with their leader's instructions, and the time moved along smoothly.

The men disappeared out the door, returning shortly with the requested materials. They placed sawhorses in appropriate locations near each end of the table, laid boards over them to create a bench, and stepped back to admire their work. "There, that should do the job," Al Weaver said.

"Yep," Uncle Ned nodded his approval.

Immediately Faith Ann and Bobby climbed over the make-shift bench and sat stiff backed and ready for dinner.

"Hey, you two," Hannah commanded, "get down from there. Dinner isn't ready yet."

"We know that," Faith Ann responded. "We was just testing it out."

"Well, get down and stay down 'til dinner's ready. Why don't you go outdoors and play?"

The kids hopped off the bench and ran outside, slamming the door with an impact that shook the whole place.

"Well . . . I told them to leave," Hannah said with a grin.

Later the family sat at Thanksgiving dinner, and Uncle Ned blessed the food. "Lord, we say thank you for all the blessings of life. May your spirit go with us throughout this day and all the days to come."

"Yes, Lord," Katherine whispered. "Thank you for our home that was saved from the fire, and please watch over Clive and make it possible for him to be here when this baby comes." She rested her hand on her abdomen, wondering what her husband was doing on this Thanksgiving Day.

CHAPTER 17

CLIVE AND JASPER sat in the cook shanty with the four Farley men, sharing a Thanksgiving dinner of roast pork, rutabagas, and beans, with vinegar pie for dessert. The boys, Dean and Eric, sat at the far end of the table, and the women worked in the kitchen with Emma. Tomorrow the Farleys would leave for their new tract of land just north of DuBois. Clive smiled to think of his family's celebration. Katherine and the girls would be spending the day with Aunt Mae and Uncle Ned. Aunt Mae would be barking orders, and everyone would be falling in line. He wondered if they had invited Adam to share the holiday. He hoped so. It was comforting to know that the young man was staying at Camp 8. It'd make things easier for Katherine to have him there.

Soon the meal was finished, and Clive made his way outside with Luc and Jasper. They walked through the camp, surveying the upcoming winter's work, discussing the potential harvest and dissecting news from the most recent *Police Gazette*.

Things were going well, and Clive became increasingly hopeful that he could get the camps organized and go home to be with his family when his child was born.

The Thanksgiving celebration had come and gone, and Katherine's life was settling back into the empty rut that it had become since her husband left for the camps. Hannah would be home until Monday afternoon, and then she'd return to County Normal. Faith Ann would go back to school, Adam would be at work, and Katherine would be alone most of the time. Just now Hannah slept with Faith Ann behind the coatroom wall, and Adam was at work.

Katherine lay abed, listening to the wind whistling around corners and rattling windows. It was going to be a nasty day, and the chickens needed to be fed before the storm got worse.

She climbed out of bed, dressed, and slipped into her overcoat and boots. Then she headed for the chicken coop, stopping in the shed for a container of grain. She held the feed under her jacket and stepped outside into the raging weather. Leaning into the wind, she made her way across the yard toward the coop. She arrived at the henhouse, reached for the latch, and pressed it upward.

Suddenly a blast of icy wind raged past. It wrenched the door out of her hand and slammed it into her side, pressing her against the building and sending the feed flying in every direction. The door flapped and banged and crashed, hammering Katherine's body as she stood pinned to the wall.

After an eternity of pummeling, the gale let up, and Katherine fell to the ground. Her shoulders ached, and her cheeks burned. Searing pain pierced her side as she looked for a handhold to lift herself off the ground—but there was none. She lay, aching with pain and consumed with terror, searching for a way to get back to the cook shanty.

Finally, she rolled onto her bulging stomach, pressed the heels of her hands into the earth, and lifted her shoulders. Pulling her legs inward, she rose onto her knees and crawled toward the building, weeping and calling out to God for help.

She moved slowly, forcing a hand and then a knee forward despite the hurt, until at last she arrived at the house, sheltered from the wind. There she dropped onto the path at the base of the porch steps. "Hannah, c'mere!" she called. "I need you!" But there was no answer. "Hannah, where are you?" The only response was the sound of the wind whistling around the tool shed. She lay staring at the door weeping, gasping for breath, and drowning in her fear. She was so near and yet so far.

Then, Katherine's eyes fell upon the stones that lay along the path. She chose a midsized missile and heaved it at the door. There was no answer so she tried again. She heaved with all her might and a loud crack announced a hit. The rock clattered across the porch and down the steps, lying inert and useless on the soil. Finally, after Katherine had tossed a dozen stones, only to have them skitter back onto the ground, the door opened, and Faith Ann stood in its breach.

Panic spread across the little girl's face. "Mama!" she screamed. "Mama!"

"Go get Hannah," Katherine hollered, and the little girl took off on the run, yelling to her sister.

Then everything went black.

"Hannah, Hannah ..." Faith Ann was pounding on her sister's side, shaking and yanking at her shirtsleeve. "Hannah, get up."

"What? What?" Hannah threw back the covers and sat upright, rubbing her eyes to clear her senses. "Faith Ann, what's all the ruckus?"

"Mama's outside," the little girl cried. "She's hurt."

In a flash Hannah threw on her robe and ran to the door. She pulled the entry open and found Katherine lying on the ground, limp and insensible.

"Katherine," Hannah screamed. She ran to her stepmother's side, grabbed her arm, and tried to lift her. "Katherine, get up!" But the woman made no move. She lay dead to the world—out cold and heavy as a rock.

"Katherine," Hannah yelled, "we gotta get you inside. You gotta get up!"

Katherine opened her eyes and looked around. She reached for Hannah.

"C'mon, Faith Ann," Hannah called. "You can help her stay steady."

Slowly, and with Katherine and Faith Ann's help, Hannah pulled her stepmother onto her knees. She lifted the woman's arm and placed it over her shoulder. Holding on with all her might, she rose and lifted her burden upright. At last Katherine flexed her muscles and put her weight onto her own feet. Hannah sighed with relief. Her stepmother was standing. Slowly but surely Katherine ascended the steps.

"Faith Ann, get the door," Hannah ordered. The little girl flung the entrance wide, and Hannah guided her stepmother through the house to the bedroom. There Katherine collapsed onto her bed—out cold.

At that point Hannah paused. She took a deep breath to calm her nerves and then she spoke slowly and clearly, exhibiting a composure she did not feel. "Faith Ann," she said. "I have to get Granny Weemes, and you have to stay here with your mama. If she wakes up, tell her where I went."

Faith Ann whimpered softly, but she nodded in agreement. Hannah left the cook shanty and hurried down the road toward Granny Weemes' house, running as fast as her legs would carry her. "Please, Granny," she wept, "you gotta be home." She grew tired, but there was no place in her plan for a break. She faltered, took several deep breaths, and plunged onward. "Just put one foot ahead of the other," she told herself. "Just put one foot ahead of the other."

With each step, the thought of what lay behind plagued her consciousness—Katherine, lying on her bed with her body smashed and broken and only Faith Ann to watch over her. The young woman's chest ached, and her legs screamed their pain. Only a little way to go . . . she could make it . . . she had to.

Finally, Hannah entered Granny's yard. She raced up the steps two at a time and hammered on the door. She didn't know what was louder, her fist pounding on the entry or the beating of her heart.

Then the portal flew open and Luke Weemes stood in the breach.

"Luke," Hannah cried. "Where's Granny? Katherine's in trouble . . . she fell and Granny's gotta come."

At that moment Granny appeared in the doorway, clad in her nightgown and peering through weary eyes. "Oh, Granny," Hannah hollered. "Katherine fell. She's hurt and you gotta come . . . now."

"Hannah, slow down," Granny said. "What happened?" Hannah stopped, took a breath, and started over. "Katherine fell. She's unconscious and all black and blue. I left her with Faith Ann."

Immediately Granny flew into action. "Luke, go get the carriage," she said. "I gotta dress and pick up my bag." The midwife disappeared into the other room as Luke ran outside.

Soon Granny reappeared with medicine bag in hand. "C'mon, Hannah," she called, and the two women hurried outside. They climbed into the carriage that stood waiting in the driveway.

Hannah's eyes filled with tears. She'd done all she could. The rest was up to Granny.

Granny put her hand on Hannah's knee. "It'll be okay. Katherine'll be just fine. We're going to fix everything."

Hannah wasn't so sure.

CHAPTER 18

NOW REMEMBER, DON'T let her out of bed for anything." With that, Granny Weemes climbed into her carriage and rode off into the afternoon, leaving Hannah alone with her new responsibility. She would be a housemaid for the duration of Katherine's pregnancy. She wouldn't go back to normal school, and she wouldn't complete her education. She fell onto the settee, weeping silently.

Then she heard a muffled whimper and looked up to see Faith Ann, standing nearby and staring at her with wide-eyed apprehension. "Hannah," the girl said, "what's the matter? Is mama okay?"

Hannah reached out to her sister. "Oh, Faith Ann," she murmured, "your mama's gonna be just fine. Granny Weemes took good care of her."

"Will she be able to get supper 'n stuff?"

Hannah looked into Faith Ann's eyes. "No, she won't be able to get supper. She needs to rest for a long time."

"But what happened? How did she get hurt?"

"We don't know, but she's okay now, and she can tell us about it after she's rested a bit."

"But who'll help us get dinner and do dishes and make the beds and stuff?"

Hannah gave her sister a quick squeeze. "I guess we'll just have to do it together. I'll be here to get meals, and we'll do the dishes together . . . and if the beds don't get made, we'll sleep in 'em anyway."

A Cheshire-cat grin spread across Faith Ann's face. "And we won't tell Mama, okay?"

"Okay, it'll be our little secret." Hannah wiped the dampness from her stepsister's cheeks.

"Can I go see Mama now?" the girl wanted to know.

"Let's take a peek. If she's awake, you can go in." Hannah led the way to the bedroom, opened the door a crack and looked inside to find Katherine lying immobile, staring at the ceiling. "Are you okay?" she said. "Faith Ann wants to come in."

Katherine turned her eyes toward her daughter and smiled. "Come on in, honey," she whispered. "Your mama's been waiting for you."

Faith Ann moved with caution into the room and stood staring at Katherine through anxious eyes. "Mama, are you gonna be all right?"

Katherine reached out to touch her daughter. "Yes, sweetheart, I'm not feeling well right now, but I'll be fine. Granny Weemes says to stay in bed, and I'll be okay."

The little girl touched her mama's arm. "Hannah said she's gonna stay here and take care of us 'til you get better. That'll be good, won't it?"

Katherine looked up at Hannah through hurting eyes. "I'm sorry," she whispered. "Maybe you can go to school another time."

Hannah responded with a quick smile that she did not feel. "It's all right," she said. "I'll contact the school, and maybe I can complete my work when you're better." With that, Katherine sighed, and her weary eyes closed in slumber.

"Let's go see what we can find for supper," Hannah said. She led Faith Ann out of the room.

In the kitchen, the young woman opened the firepot, shoved in a couple of sticks, and reached for a bowl. "I think we'll have beef pot pie for supper tonight," she said. She opened a jar of beef stew and poured it into a baking pan. She made biscuit dough, spread it over the top, and put it in the oven to bake.

Faith Ann reached for the plates and silver that Hannah placed on the cabinet. "I'll set the table."

So the world changed, and Hannah was no longer a student. She was a homemaker with her little sister as her support. She'd make it. She had to.

Later the door opened and Adam entered. "Mmmmmm, smells good in here," he called. He'd been sharing the evening meal regularly since Clive's departure. He hung his coat on a nail and looked around. "Where's Katherine?"

"Mama fell and got hurt," Faith Ann blurted. "She's gotta stay in bed."

Adam's brow shot upward. "Really bad, huh?

"That's right," Hannah said. "She went out to feed the chickens, and the henhouse door got caught by the wind. It slammed into her, and she couldn't get up." The young woman shot a conspiratorial glance at Adam and mouthed the word, "Later."

Adam nodded, and the family took their places for the evening meal. "Faith Ann, it's your turn," Hannah said.

The little girl bowed her head. "Thank you for this food and bless it to our good," she said.

Hannah waited for the "amen," but it didn't come. Finally she looked up to see her little sister with hands doubled into fists, rubbing her eyes with her knuckles. "And help Mama to get better," the girl said at last. Faith Ann brushed her hand over her wet cheeks and looked up.

Later that evening Hannah walked with Adam to the men's shanty. "Katherine's okay for now," she said. "But Granny Weemes says she can't get out of bed. And, of course, that means I won't be going back to normal school."

"Oh Hannah, I'm sorry."

Hannah's lips drew into a thin line. "Maybe I can go to school next year, but that means I won't be able to replace Verena—and I won't have money to help with finances around here."

Adam brushed his hand across Hannah's back. Hannah leaned close to absorb his masculine support. She stayed with Adam, visiting until the pain eased. Then she went back to Faith Ann and Katherine and to her new duties as homemaker and nursemaid.

Seth stood looking over the Farleys' new site. Tall pines reached upward on all sides with a small creek beginning from a spring that flowed out of the hilly terrain. It was about as remote as one could imagine—perfect for his situation.

"All right, boys," Max called. "Let's get this cabin rolled up." The man flicked the reins, the horses moved toward the logs that were decked nearby, and Seth tailed down the first log.

Immediately Wade toggled it to the whiffletree, and Max flicked the reins. The horses leaned in, hauling the first girder to the shanty site. There Max released the chain, and the log dropped onto the ground. Seth and Wade maneuvered it into place, while Ike cut notches at each end to make a corner coupling and Max returned for another section.

Soon the base for the shanty was laid—a rectangle about thirty feet wide by thirty-four feet long. Wade and Seth and Eric and Dean packed dirt along its sides to hold it in place.

At that point Ike and Wade placed poles against the base, creating a ramp to roll each successive timber into position. Max hauled logs for a second tier, and the younger men maneuvered them into place. Thus the work went on. By evening, the walls were complete, and everyone slept, fully dressed, on the floor in a roofless building.

Over several days the Farleys added a roof to the main shanty, packed cracks with swamp moss, and chinked them with long v-shaped strips of wood to keep out the wind. Lastly, the strips of chinking were covered with mud to complete a seal. The building was complete.

The kitchen range would come in on the tote wagon in a few days. Bunks, tables, and other furniture would be handmade as time permitted.

A new camp had taken form in the deep woods.

Adam sat on the cook shanty porch, listening to the sound of the croaking frogs and chirping crickets. An owl hooted in the distance, calling out to his friends. The world was at peace.

Then as he sat mulling over the crossroads of his life, Hannah stepped outside and stood leaning against the porch rail, gazing into the night.

"It sure is beautiful out here, isn't it?" Adam said.

The young woman turned and took a seat on a nearby chair. "Mmmmhmm."

Adam waited several minutes and then he spoke. "Hannah," he said. "There's something I've been meaning to talk to you about."

"Oh?"

"I'm thinking about going to the camps with Clive when he comes home at Christmas time."

"What are you talking about?" Hannah responded. "Why? Clive gets around to all the camps. He's the one who'll have the best chance to find Seth."

Adam shook his head. "But Clive has never met Seth. Seth could walk right past Clive, and he'd never know it."

The air grew quiet. "But we need you here, and besides, what about your job? Have you talked to Sam about this?"

"I haven't talked to Sam, but I'm sure he'd let me go. Things are slow these days with so many men gone to the camps."

A long pause ensued and Hannah responded. "I suppose you're right," she replied, "but I don't have to like it." As she turned to go, she reached into her pocket and pulled out two letters. "Here, post these tomorrow, will you?" She slid the mail into the young man's hand. "We need to let the school know that I won't be coming back, and Clive needs to know about Katherine's condition."

Adam took the letters and tucked them into his pocket. "I'm sorry it turned out this way, Hannah."

Hannah sighed. "It'll be okay. We have to do what we have to do." She reached for the door. "And I better get back inside."

"Okay." Adam rose and descended the porch steps. "Goodnight," he called. He made his way toward the tool shed, with his mind awhirl. His heart ached for this girl that he cared deeply about.

CHAPTER 19

CLIVE SAT WITH Molly Walker at Rifkin Camp, drinking coffee and reminiscing about life. Winter snows had begun in earnest, and ice roads that were used to haul timber to lakes and rivers were in process. Soon the woods would be etched with frozen trails—routes designed to hasten a host of gigantic logs on their way to market. Then, barring unforeseen circumstances, Clive would return to his pregnant wife and unborn child. "Molly," he said, "do you ever feel deserted out here, living apart from the rest of the world?"

Molly sighed, looking out the window at the isolated environs that were so much a part of her world. "Well . . ." a long pause filled the air, "yes, there are times when I think about quilting parties and community dinners and stuff, but I'm okay. We have our garden, and we keep busy canning and tending animals and things. During the winter, there are the jacks that come by regularly, so it's not so bad. We're not completely cut off from everything."

As she spoke, wagon wheels creaked outside, and the tote master's voice reverberated on the air, cursing and chastising the animals that had ferried him there. "Whoa, you worthless old nags," he yelled.

"Burgess," Molly called, "the tote wagon is here." Molly's husband emerged from a back room and joined his wife and Clive. Together they made their way outside to welcome Gabby Helms and his transport.

"Whoa, you rundown hunks of crow bait," Gabby shouted. The wagon came to a halt in front of the cook shanty, and the wizened old man tossed the reins over the buckboard. Then he bounded onto the ground, stretching his thin and hardened torso to its limits.

"Well, Molly," he called out, "I'm hungry. What-a-ya got to eat?"

"Shoe-pack pie, you grizzly old man," Molly responded. "Vinegar 'n all."

"Sounds good to me," Gabby responded. "Set 'er up, woman, and we'll be there as soon as we can."

"Just hold your tongue, old man," Molly responded. She grinned, belying the tone in her voice, and went inside to prepare the meal.

With that Gabby climbed aboard the wagon and heaved provisions over the side to the men—fifty-pound bags of flour and sugar and coffee, oats for the horses, and a bolt of cloth for Molly. Last of all he reached under the driver's seat for the mailbag and handed it to Burgess.

Burgess turned and carried the leather sack into the cook shanty. Piece by piece he sorted through the mail. There were magazines, envelopes, and packages, but nothing for Rifkin Camp—or for Waterhouse, for that matter. "Hey, Gabby," Burgess said. "This stuff is for Loughlin. There's not a thing here for Waterhouse."

"What?" Gabby reached for the bag, scanning its contents. "Egad," he spat. "Those morons over in Boyne City would lose their heads if they wasn't fastened on." The man turned and lugged the container outside. "Snivelin' idiots," he sputtered. Apparently it didn't occur to the man that it was he who had picked up the wrong satchel. He threw it onto the tote wagon with a slam.

As the container hit the wagon's floor, the thump reverberated on the air, and disappointment settled on Clive's core. There was no letter from Katherine. He walked away empty-hearted and wondering about his family. Was everything all right? Were Katherine and the girls strong and healthy? Had their needs been met?

Hannah reached for the letter Adam held out to her and scanned the envelope. She noted the words in the upper left corner and swallowed the pain in her chest. *Boyne City Normal School, Boyne City Michigan.* She slipped her thumb under the flap, tore open the letter, and began to read.

Dear Miss McLean,
We are sorry to hear of your stepmother's illness and your inability to return to school. We have examined your records, however, and it appears that you could finish the work at home if you desire. At your request, we will send the uncompleted lessons to the local schoolteacher. She can oversee the completion of your studies, and you can graduate with your class. Please check with Miss Verena Spencer for further information and let us know of your desire.
   Harold Hampton
   Dean of Studies
   County Normal School: Boyne City, Michigan

Tears of joy welled in Hannah's eyes as she handed the open letter to Adam. She turned her back to hide her emotions.

"Fantastic!" Adam said as he completed the reading. He thrust both thumbs into the air. "I've been praying for something like this. Let's go tell Katherine."

"Yes, let's." Hannah led the way to Katherine's room, where her stepmother lay staring at the ceiling, and handed her the post. "Oh Hannah," Katherine said as she scanned the letter. "That's perfect; it worked out OK after all."

"I'll go see Verena tomorrow," Hannah responded, "right after Faith Ann comes home from school."

The next day passed on turtle time. Hannah milked old Maudie, fixed breakfast, and sent Faith Ann off to school. She did dishes and then checked the clock. It was 9:30. She fed the chickens, made the bed, and swept the floor, working until noon. A half-day had passed. She went to the cellar, chose a jar of mulligan stew, and warmed it for lunch. After lunch, she washed the dishes and put them away. About one o'clock, she noticed that a container of souring cream on the cabinet was ready to churn. She poured it into a two quart jar, took a seat on the settee, and began to churn it into butter. She tipped the container this way and that until her arms grew tired, and still she worked. She moved the container back and forth and up and down and to and fro until she felt her arms must fall off, yet she continued to shake the jar.

At last Hannah could see blobs of butter forming from the contents. She poured off the buttermilk, washed the pale yellow mass with cold water, and began to knead it. When the little bubbles of whey were dispersed, she added a bit of salt, put the finished product into a bowl, and took it to the cellar. It was still only two o'clock.

Returning to the living room, Hannah picked up her pillowcase and went to work, embroidering one end of the linen sack with a picture—a little girl, watering the garden with a water pot.

Finally, the door opened, and Faith Ann entered, slamming it in her wake. "Faith Ann, how many times have I told you not to slam that door?" Hannah said.

"I'm sorry," the little girl wailed. "I didn't mean to slam it. It just banged shut." The child scrambled out of her boots, hung her coat on a nail, and ran toward the kitchen.

"Anyway, I'm glad you're here," Hannah went on. "You gotta stay with your mama, because I'm going to see Miss Verena."

Faith Ann turned, looking at her big sister with eyes wide. "I didn't do anything bad."

"It's okay," Hannah said. "But c'mere a minute. I have something to tell you."

Faith Ann's face transformed into a pout. "I didn't do anything. .It was Mary Ann's fault."

Hannah reached out to her little sister. "This is not about you or anything you've done."

Faith Ann wiped her eyes and came near.

"I got a letter from my school today," Hannah said, "and they tell me I can go to school right here in Hitchcock. Miss Verena can be my teacher."

Faith Ann's face lit up. "You mean we'll go to school together?"

"Well, not exactly." Hannah reached for her coat. "I'll have to wait until you get home, so you can take care of your mama while I'm gone."

"Oh," the little girl said. "Okay, I'll take care of Mama, and you can go to school."

"So let's go tell her." Hannah led the way to Katherine's bedroom.

"Guess what, Mama," Faith Ann said as they entered. "Miss Verena's gonna be Hannah's teacher, and I'm gonna stay here with you."

"Yes," Katherine responded. "Hannah told me about it. I'm sure you'll be a good caretaker."

Hannah donned her coat and boots, exiting the cook shanty, barely aware of that last comment. As she walked down Birch Lake Road, she thought about her upcoming conversation with Verena. Maybe she'd walk into the school and say, "Hey Verena, guess what." Or she could say something like, "Did you get a letter from Boyne City?" Probably she'd just hand the letter to the teacher and let her read it.

CHAPTER 20

KATHERINE LAY IN her bed, waiting for time to pass. She'd been having false labor for some time now, and she was sure the child would deliver soon. Where was Clive?

She reached for the novel on the bedside table and let it fall on the blankets, unopened. She was certain she'd read every book in the county six or seven times, and she wasn't convinced that she cared whether Anna Whiting fell off the hay wagon and broke her leg.

Then Hannah came into the room and handed her the mail. There was a copy of the *Police Gazette*, a letter from the County Wide Farmer's Association, and a reminder of the upcoming New Year's dance at the grange . . . and a letter from Clive.

Dear Katherine,

Things here are pretty much as you would expect. Most of the bosses have completed their plans for skid roads and are beginning to hire jacks for the season. Every day men come through on their way to this camp or that. Luc DuBois is

*especially popular for his tough leadership that is tempered
with fairness.*

*I haven't gotten any mail from home because the mailbags
got mixed up. How are things? I think of my family every day,
and I'm missing you and the girls.
Hope all is well.*

Clive

Katherine put the letter aside. Clive hadn't received her post,
and he didn't know she'd hurt herself. Nor did he know the baby
could come early. She leaned back, waiting for time to pass and
wishing for an escape from that cursed bed. "Please, God," she
prayed, "send Clive home." The only response was emptiness in
her soul. She lay counting the minutes until suppertime.

Then at last, Hannah appeared in the doorway carrying a
tray with her meal.

Katherine had long ago realized she couldn't lie perfectly still
as Granny Weemes had suggested, and with Hannah's help, she
propped herself onto a couple of pillows. "Thank you, Hannah,"
she said. "You've been a perfect angel. I don't know how I could
ever repay you."

"It worked out all right," Hannah responded. "I'm getting
my schooling right here in Hitchcock, and we can be together as
a family." Hannah smiled and left the room.

Katherine returned to her life of waiting—staring at the ceiling and wishing for an afternoon in the sun. It had been her life
for weeks, and it would continue to be so for some time to come.
An hour passed, and then another and another, until at last daylight began to ebb and evening shades teetered on the horizon.
Where was Clive? What was he doing? Katherine sighed and
rolled over, waiting for time to pass.

Then, just as she edged onto her shoulder, she heard the cook
shanty door open. A shriek rattled the entire house, as Hannah's
voice resonated on the air. "Clive!"

Katherine sprang from her mattress and ran full speed into
her husband's arms, nestling in his embrace. Moments later
Clive stepped back. "Hey, what's going on here?" he said. "Why
are you in your nightgown?"

"Oh Clive, so much has happened since you left. I got smashed by the chicken coop door, we called Granny Weemes, but the baby wasn't hurt, and Hannah couldn't go to school because I couldn't get out of bed. Finally the school sent her lessons to Verena, so that worked out all right, but I'm still in bed." The words spilled from Katherine's mouth without a break.

Incredulity filled Clive's face. "What? How?"

Suddenly Katherine realized she had abandoned her cage and violated Granny Weemes orders. "C'mon, I gotta go back to bed." She turned and led the way back to her imprisonment. Her family followed and Clive took a seat by her side.

"Granny Weemes said Mama had to stay in bed," Faith Ann interjected. "And I took care of her some of the time."

"And I can see you did a fine job." Clive patted his daughter's shoulder and turned to Katherine. "So what are you doing in bed?" Katherine went over the events of the past weeks, finishing with her confinement and the many long hours of waiting for her life to return to normal.

Without a word, Hannah reached out for Faith Ann's hand and the girls left the room, leaving Katherine alone with her husband.

Clive sat silent, gazing at his wife with adoring eyes. When he spoke again, his love colored every word. "I missed you," he whispered. "I'm so sorry for all the worry, but I'm here now, and we'll be okay."

"Yes, we'll be okay." Whatever the future held, Katherine's dear one was at her side, and she would be fine.

It was New Year's Eve, and Clive stood with his family near the old pump at Camp 8. "Thirty seconds to go," Hannah said, and the man lifted his gun to his shoulder. His muscles tensed as he rested his forefinger on the trigger. "Twenty seconds, ten seconds, five, four, three, two—now!" The sound of celebration ricocheted across the land. Firearms blasted across the entire community, and shouts of joy emanated on the air.

"Happy New Year!" Clive shouted. "Happy New Year!" the family responded. There was laughing and shouting and clapping. Finally, Clive led the way inside, where they gathered around Katherine's bed to celebrate with cider, donuts, and the cookies that Hannah had made especially for the occasion. They laughed and talked for at least a half hour. Then as the excitement of the day dwindled, Hannah led a sleepy Faith Ann to their bed, and Adam headed for the tool shed. Clive found his place beside his wife, resting his hand on her stomach. When the child moved within, he whispered, "How are you feeling, Mama?"

"Mmmm," Katherine murmured. "I'm feeling fine now that you're here."

"Have you picked a name?"

"I think we should name him Clifford after his Grandpa Isaman."

"And what if he's a girl?"

"Oh, he's a boy." Katherine assured her husband. "Granny Weemes did the swinging needle test, and the pin swung sideways."

"Oh, I see." Clive snuggled close to his wife, and there he fell asleep, dreaming of baby boys and toy trucks and of hunting excursions with a young son.

Then just a few hours later he awoke to a soft moan coming from the other side of the bed. His wife lay beside him—straining. "Katherine, are you okay?" he whispered.

"Yes," she responded, "but I've been having pains for about an hour now. I think the baby's coming."

"What?" Clive sprang from the bed. "I'll go get Granny Weemes."

"No," Katherine said, reaching for his hand. "Send Hannah. I want you here."

"Okay, but let's get moving." He threw on his clothes and made his way to Hannah's room. He laid his hand on his stepdaughter's arm. "Hannah," he whispered, "wake up." Gently he shook the girl's shoulder. "C'mon, Hannah, you gotta go get Granny Weemes."

Hannah roused and looked up at her stepfather through squinty eyes. "What's 'a matter?"

"Katherine's in labor," Clive whispered. "You gotta go get Granny Weemes."

Hannah's eyes flew open. "The baby's coming?"

Clive nodded and held his finger to his lips. "Shhhhh, don't wake Faith Ann."

"Okay, okay, I'm coming." Clive left the room as Hannah threw back the covers.

Then as the young woman donned her coat, Faith Ann appeared in the doorway, sleepy-eyed and stumbling over herself. "What's 'a matter?" she moaned. "Where's Hannah going?"

Clive put his arm around his daughter's shoulders. "Mama's got a tummy ache," he said, "and Hannah's going to get some help."

Hannah disappeared outside into the darkness.

Clive patted Faith Ann's shoulder and led her back to her room behind the wall. He tucked her in, kissed her, and left the room.

Returning to the bedroom, Clive found Katherine panting and straining. "They're coming every three minutes now," she said. "And they're coming hard."

"Hold on," Clive said. "Granny's coming." Clive was a weathered woodsman. He'd worked with the roughest and toughest of lumberjacks, yet visceral jelly shivered in his stomach. He searched his mind, trying to remember what his pa used to do when delivering calves. "Make sure they get to breathing and tie the cord," his pa had said.

"Oohhh," Katherine moaned, and a stream of dampness oozed its way through the bedding. She breathed in short gasps and lay panting.

Clive's heart throbbed in his chest. *C'mon, Hannah,* he thought. *You gotta get Granny Weemes right away. C'mon, Granny Weemes, we need you before this baby arrives.*

Then it happened.

"Oooohhh," Katherine cried. "I can't wait. It's coming." With a gasp, she threw back the covers. "You're going to have to catch it." Drawing on his lumberman's grit, Clive stepped near the bed.

He stood transfixed, watching for his child to appear. Then, without any effort on Clive's part, his son emerged into time and space. A baby boy dropped into his hands.

Immediately Granny Weemes appeared in the doorway, and Clive almost cried. "I think I just delivered my son," he stammered.

"Okay." Granny Weemes said. "Get some surgical scissors from my bag and stand by for further orders."

Clive stood awestruck as the midwife took his son and dropped him onto Katherine's stomach. He provided tools as the old woman requested and gave general assistance to help with the remaining work. Then he left the room and fell onto the sofa in a stupor. He'd survived the most frightening moment of his entire life.

Several hours later, Katherine was lying with her little boy beside her in the bed when Clive entered with Faith Ann in tow. "Come in, sweetheart," Katherine called. "Come see your new baby brother. His name is Cliffy."

Faith Ann came near and stood looking down at the child. She reached out and touched Cliffy's hand, and he curled his tiny fingers around his big sister's pinky. A broad grin crossed the girl's face. Then she touched his cheek. "Look, he has curly hair just like me."

"Yes," Katherine said, "he has curly hair from his daddy, just like you."

A contemplative frown crossed Faith Ann's face for a second and then she grinned. "My baby brother looks like me."

CHAPTER 21

I T WAS A cold Saturday afternoon in early January, and Adam stood in the tool shed, looking out at the frozen world of Camp 8. A heavy winter snow had fallen, and the ground glistened in an icy panorama of white. He thought about Clive's upcoming return to the camps, and his heart beat fast with the decision he'd made. He needed to tell Clive about going to the woods, and he needed to do it soon.

As he sat considering his options, the door opened, and Clive entered, carrying a box of Christmas decorations. "Hey, Adam," he said. "How are things?" He deposited the package onto a shelf and turned.

"Not too bad," the young man replied. He took a deep breath and moved toward his host. "Clive," he said, "there's something I need to talk to you about."

"Yes?" Clive stood with eyebrows raised, waiting.

"I've been thinking about the search for Seth, and I think I should go to the camps with you."

Clive's face broke into a grin. "I can't believe you just said that. I've been thinking the same thing. The fact is, I don't know

Seth. You might see things that I would miss. But how about Sam? Have you talked to him about this?"

"Yes." Adam nodded. "Things are slow right now anyway. Sam just clapped me on the back and said goodbye."

"Okay." Clive reached out for Adam's hand. "The deal is done.

We'll head out together in a few days."

That night Adam packed his turkey. He found an old pillowcase and ran a rope through the hem. Then he gathered his belongings, some heavy winter underwear, some wool socks, and a couple of flannel and wool shirts, because temperatures in the woods could fall well below zero. He packed a small sack with soap and other simple necessities and showed it to Clive.

Clive thumbed through it and pronounced it ready.

Hannah stood on the porch in the crisp January air, looking up at the stars and wondering what sort of universe lay out there. Were there really messages in those nightlights? Could stargazers really tell what was to come just by the location of those glowing dots? She pulled her jacket close around her midriff and leaned against the rail, listening to the creak of the rocking chair as Katherine rocked little Cliffy to sleep.

Looking across the field, she could see the Weavers' farm, barely visible in the evening mist. That house had once been hers. She smiled with the remembrance. She'd been at odds with Katherine at the time, and she could hardly believe her ears when her stepmother accepted her suggestion and moved into the place. They'd appropriated the house without permission from anyone. Then as she sat remembering, the door opened and closed behind her. Footsteps echoed softly on the planking, moving nearer in the twilight. Turning, she saw Adam at her elbow, and a sense of peace entered her soul. How could she have taken umbrage at this young man when they first met . . . before she'd even made his acquaintance?

The two stood together in silence, considering the beauty of creation and the splendor of the world. "It's a beautiful evening," Adam whispered. The words filtered into the air as soft and gentle as the night.

"Mmmhmmm," Hannah answered. A tremble reverberated through her torso with the sense of his nearness.

"Hannah," Adam whispered. "I'm leaving for the camps tomorrow."

"Yes, and we'll miss you." She could feel the young man's arm resting on the post behind her, and without realizing it, she leaned toward him.

Then his arm left the post and found its way to her waist. "Hannah, do you think you could ever care for me?"

His presence filled her torso with warmth, and her breath came softly. She turned and looked into his face, sensing a bond she'd never known before. She looked up into the most loving eyes she'd ever seen.

Adam pulled her close, and his lips met hers—ever so gently at first and then with a yearning that spoke louder than words. She gave herself to his embrace and the two melded into one —alone in a universe where only their relationship was an issue.

Two days later Adam left for the deep woods.

It was a warm Sunday afternoon, and Seth sat on the codgers' bench with the Farley men. A distant wail announced the passing of a train somewhere in the north as Ike strummed his guitar. Seth leaned against the building with eyes closed and hands clasped at the back of his neck. He sat reveling in the sun's warmth. The world was at peace.

He sighed and opened his eyes to see a tall strapping Indian. "Well," Max said, "here comes Tom Running Fox. I reckon we'll have a visitor for a day or two."

"Yep," Ike went on, "and we'll get some stuff done around here." Ike and Max rose to greet their visitor.

"Farleys," Tom said as he came near, "I come see . . . maybe need help."

"I'm sure there's stuff around here you can do," Max responded. "You just sit down here with us, and we'll talk about it."

"Thank Farleys," the big Indian said. "But Tom go make place for self in hay." The man walked away, striding toward the barn on his long, lanky legs with his pack on his back.

Seth turned to Wade. "Who is that?"

"Name's Tom Running Fox," Wade responded. "I don't know too much about him except that he shows up every now and then. He does whatever work he's assigned, eats at our table, and sleeps in the haymow. Then one day he just walks away."

"Seems strange," Seth said.

"Yes, but he can be a big help, and all the camps invite him in. I guess his tribe kicked him out or something."

Seth's heart reached out to a man who, like himself, had no home and no place to go.

CHAPTER 22

ADAM STOOD IN the camp office with Clive, looking up at the biggest man he'd ever seen.

"Luc," Clive said to the man, "this is Adam Beste. He's been staying in the men's shanty at my place, and he's looking for a job."

"Well now," the man said, "what can you do, young man? You know anything about life in the woods?"

"Actually, I haven't been in the camps before," Adam responded. "But I'm a good worker. I lived on a farm all my life, and I can pile brush or shovel snow or do whatever you may need. I learn fast, and I'm willing to do what I need to do."

"All right then, we'll start you out swampin'. We'll put you to work with Harold Bosun tomorrow. He'll take you to the site, and you'll cut branches from fallen trees and clear space for hauling. In the meantime, I suggest you settle in and get some rest."

Abruptly, the door flew open, and a wiry little man with a shaggy beard and gray hair that stuck out in all directions entered. "Someone's a-messin' with my tools again," he hollered. "If I ever catch that critter, I'll knock his block off."

Luc DuBois stepped forward. "I don't know where your tools are, Jake, but I have a job for you."

Jake scowled and mumbled something under his breath as Luc made introductions. "Jake, this is Adam. I want you to take him to the men's shanty and find him a bunk."

The man squinted his eyes and gave Adam the once over. "I dunno," he said. "You look pretty puny to me. C'n ya hold yer own in a bar fight?"

Luc DuBois threw a scowl at the little man that would scare the fleas off a wild dog. "Just don't let me find any of that rotgut in this camp," he thundered.

"No boss, not here," Jake responded. He turned and led Adam outside.

Adam felt a little nonplussed, but he followed Jake. "There's the men's shanty." The man pointed toward a large building on the north end of the camp. It was made of logs and had a single door in the end with a small window on each side. "So, what's a snivelin' little runt like you doin' out here in this God-forsaken place anyway?" Jake spat. The man shuffled along, spitting tobacco juice into the snow with every step or two.

Adam paused in surprise. "I needed a job."

"Well, you got one all right." The man shot a streak of tobacco juice out the side of his mouth, striking the men's shanty wall and leaving a stream of spittle running down its front. "Hollow-headed varmints won't leave my stuff alone, and the boss won't do nothin' about it," he muttered. He pulled open the door and led the way inside where a row of bunks stretched the full length of the room on either side. Mats of straw, that were by this time mashed and broken, served as mattresses. A bench was attached to each of the beds for seating.

Jake tramped along the length of the room and pointed to a wooden bunk squeezed against the wall. "That'll be your bed right there," he said. "Stash yer turkey at the foot, and make yerself at home."

Adam tossed the pillowcase onto the bunk. "Thank you, Jake."

The old man turned. "And be careful not to spill the hog-wash," he said. Jake pulled his scotch cap over his ears and exited the building, chuckling under his breath. Adam didn't remember coming across any hogwash to spill but if he heard of any, he'd be careful not to get caught up in it.

After the man left, Adam retrieved his comb and mirror from his turkey, laid them on a ledge near the head of the bed, and sat peering around in the semidarkness.

A large steel heater stood in the center of the room with a wire above it that stretched from one side of the area to the other. Wet and smelly socks hung from the line, along with mittens and pants and other disagreeable items, mingling their aroma with the smell of cramped and unwashed bodies. The place reeked with an unholy stench that permeated the very boards that made up the walls.

There were two doors, the one in front through which Adam had entered, and one in back with a large vat nearby. Clive had said the DuBois camp was exceptional in that it had a laundry tub and that few of the camps had either a back door or a wash-tub—but Luc DuBois, it was said, went the extra mile for his men.

The young man lay on his cot, allowing his mind to wander back to Camp 8. He thought about Hannah and her compelling smile that had attracted him from the day he'd noticed her at the church, and he thought of the months he'd spent trying to reach past the wall she'd built between them. Then he remembered Torrie's Spring and the breakthrough that had begun their friendship, and he thought about that last night with Hannah, the clean fresh air, the rush of her presence, and the warmth of her lips.

Suddenly an image flared in his mind, and his heart broke. Seth was out here somewhere, running from himself.

What had Adam done—standing there with his best friend's sister, holding her close and reveling in her touch, while Seth hid from the world? Adam must find the young man before he himself would be free to love. He sighed and exited the building, hoping to find Clive and visit a bit before the walker left camp.

As he stepped outside Clive was coming his way. "Well, what do you think?" the man said as he came near.

"I guess I'll make it," Adam responded. "Though it's pretty smelly in there. Do you ever get used to it?"

"I guess they do. They stay there all winter," Clive responded. "I usually sleep in the office, so I don't have to deal with it." Clive paused and looked around. Then he nodded. "Hey, let's go to the cook shanty for coffee."

Adam and Clive made their way toward a large building in the center of the camp. They entered and found Jasper and Jake sitting with Gabby Helms and some of the in-camp crew at the long dining table. Gabby Helms was holding forth, as usual, with a longwinded tale of the woods.

"It was a terrible sight," Gabby declared. "That load of logs ran up on old Meanie and his workmate like a bloodsuckin' monster after his lunch. The horses screamed like a couple o' bats out o' hell. I betcha the folks clear down in Kalkaska was troubled by their screamin'."

Adam and Clive found places at the table and Emma poured coffee.

"Those horses, they didn't have a chance. They took one last leap for freedom, an' stuff went a-flyin' inta space—brush, logs, sleighs, and horses exploded into one big storm. And it all landed in a heap." Gabby smashed his fist into his palm.

"After a few minutes old Meanie stood and looked around, but that young new piebald, he never did get up. He lay deader'n a doornail, while old Meanie trotted off to the barn. It was all over, and another load came a humpin' up the hill."

Adam left the cook shanty and headed to the men's quarters, where he'd spend the night. He grinned at the thought of Gabby and his stories. The man could spin a yarn like no other.

Later Adam found himself in a stinky bunk, holding his nose and scratching at the bugs that infested his bed, but it was okay. He was going to find Seth.

CHAPTER 23

EVENING WAS COMING on and Seth wandered along the river's edge with Eric and Dean. As they walked, Eric bent, picked up a stone, and threw it into the water, watching as the ripples emanated across the surface. Dean followed suit, and soon the boys were competing for the longest pitch. Seth paused to allow the boys their fun, and as he did, Max and Ike approached.

"Jeb," Max said as they came near, "we think you need to stay here with Tom Running Fox tomorrow. He'll be cleaning the barn and mending harnesses and stuff, and you can help with organization."

Seth's brow lifted in surprise. "Sure, whatever you want is fine with me." The two men walked away.

The next morning after the Farleys left for the forest, Seth and Tom Running Fox gathered supplies and made their way to the outbuilding. They cleaned mangers and then cleared refuse from the stalls, refreshing them with clean straw. As they worked, Seth approached the subject that had been on his mind from the beginning. "Running Fox," he said, "how do you come to be in the camps? Surely you have a home or a tribe where you belong." A sad smile overspread Running Fox's face. "Pa, he be trapper," the man said. "Braves, they know him, 'cause he go villages and see Indians. He be Indians' friend. Sometimes give people meat."

"But white man, he get hurt in woods, and braves, they find man sick and 'sleep. Indian take white man to village. Squaw, she get man well and he get squaw." Tom pointed to his chest. "Squaw get papoose. White man not like that."

Seth tossed a forkful of straw onto the floor and spread it about for cover.

"Pa, he leave." Tom shook his head. "Come back sometime, talk squaw, but not talk papoose."

"But that doesn't mean you can't live with your people," Seth said.

A wistful air crossed Tom's face. "No, Pa he leave tribe. Tribe, they no like squaw some more. Think white man wife be bad person. No want she be near."

Seth's heart twisted into a knot. How could a man do that to his family? This Indian's father had deserted him while he was still a baby. The boy grew to manhood knowing his dad left the tribe rather than live with his own son. Revulsion overspread the young man's soul.

"So I leave," Running Fox said. "Just go 'round in woods. Be a helper. White man like that."

Seth shook his head in commiseration. Running Fox was his brother—the man had no place to go. He just wandered through the woods, looking for a place to lay his head.

Three days later Running Fox walked away, going nowhere in a desolate world. Was that what the future held for Seth?

Hannah lay in her bed curled around Faith Ann for warmth and with two heavy quilts pulled over her shoulders. In the dining room, the stove had been banked for the night, and there were probably a few coals waiting to be urged into flame. But the space behind the wall, where Hannah and Faith Ann slept, was as cold as ice. Hannah had no desire to embark into the early morning.

She lay wondering about her brother. What was he doing? Did he have a friend? Did he ever think about coming home? She knew he was out there somewhere and that Adam would do all he could to find him, but it didn't dispel the sense of emptiness that gnawed at her heart.

She cuddled closer to Faith Ann, and the kiss she'd shared with Adam filtered into her mind. What could have possessed her to let that happen? If there was anything she didn't need, it was an affair with that man. She'd be his ally as long as Seth was in trouble, but she wouldn't fall in love with him. Still, she couldn't deny the flutter of her heart when he held her close. Hannah listened as the air resonated with the clunk of metal against metal. Katherine was in the kitchen fixing breakfast.

The young woman pushed back the covers, did a flying leap into her clothes, and headed for the dining room. Impelled by the cold, she yanked open the door to the heater and poked at the ashes that lay on the grate. Good, the coals were still hot. She reached for some kindling, piled several sticks on the embers, and added a couple of larger logs. She blew on the tinder, and the flames ignited.

As the fire flickered into life and heat began to flow into the room, Hannah went to waken Faith Ann. "C'mon, sleepyhead," she said. "You gotta get ready for school." The little girl pushed back the covers and climbed out of bed, rubbing her eyes to dispel the slumber. She grabbed her clothing and ran for the kitchen. By now the range would have produced some heat, and the room would be fairly comfortable. Hannah followed her sister and found Katherine standing over the cook-stove.

Katherine poured three pancakes onto the griddle and stood watching the bubbling batter for the exact moment to flip them onto the other side. Then as she stood waiting, Cliffy began to cry, and Hannah and Faith Ann were left to finish preparing breakfast. Hannah flipped the flapjacks while Faith Ann set the table.

Finally the meal was prepared, and Katherine came to eat while nursing Cliffy.

Hannah and Faith Ann took their places, and Katherine said grace. A big empty vacuum marked the space where Clive and Adam should have been. It would be this way until spring.

It was late afternoon, and Katherine sat in the rocking chair with Cliffy in her arms. The creak of wooden rockers lulled her toward dreamland, and an image filtered into her mind. She thought of Cliffy's birth and Clive's act of heroism. How appropriate that he had actually caught his child as the boy emerged.

Faith Ann's delivery had been a very different experience, with a midwife's careful oversight of the entire event, but lacking the child's father. She thought about Frank McLean and his love for her and for her baby, despite its irregular conception. Her love for Frank McLean nestled in the back of her soul—a love lost long ago. She pulled her baby close and peeked under the blanket to see his eyes closed in sleep.

Just then Faith Ann came flying into the shanty, slamming the door behind her and tossing her coat onto the couch.

"Faith Ann," Katherine said. "You slammed the door again. I've told you not to do that. You'll wake up little Cliffy. Now hang up your coat."

"Okay, Mama," Faith Ann said as she slithered out of her snow pants, dropping them onto the floor. "Mama," she said, "what's the difference between a pa and a daddy?"

"First, you hang up your snowsuit, young lady. Then we'll talk about daddies."

Faith Ann dragged her snowsuit across the room and took care of it. Then she came skipping back to her mother.

"Wait a minute," Katherine said. She rose and made her way to the bedroom, where she put Cliffy in his bed. Then she returned to the dining room and took a seat on the couch beside her little girl. "Now then," she said, "what's the problem?"

Faith Ann stood looking at her mother with confusion on her face. "Mama," she said, "Harold Flack's pa came to school today, and Harold called him Daddy. I told him that was wrong and the man was his pa, but he said that's what his folks told him, and they were right. Who's right, him or me?"

Katherine smiled and drew her little girl close. "Well, you're both right, so don't worry about it," she said. "It just depends on what you learned when you were little."

Faith Ann stepped back. "But you told me you were my mama, and Pa was my pa."

"Well, you see," Katherine took a seat on the couch and pulled her little girl onto the cushion beside her, "Harold's folks are immigrants. They came from England like I did, and people over there call their folks Mama and Daddy. So that's what his ma and pa taught him to say—just like I taught you to say Mama because that's what I was taught when I was a little girl."

"Harold says if you're my mama, then Mr. Clive is my daddy. He says that's just the way it is."

"Well, don't worry about it. Harold can call his folks whatever is right for them, and you can call us what's right for you."

"Oh, so you're still my mama, and Mr. Clive's my . . ." The little girl's brow furrowed, "Mr. Clive's my . . . can I have some bread and jam?"

"Sure." Katherine followed her daughter to the kitchen. She pulled a knife out of the cabinet drawer, cut a slice of bread, and spread it with apple jelly. Then she poured a glass of milk and set it on the table. "There you go," she said. Her little girl was satisfied for the moment.

CHAPTER 24

ADAM LAY ON his bunk in the men's shanty considering his search for Seth when the door opened and a troop of rough-looking men entered. A few stopped to wash up in the community basin near the doorway but most scattered toward the bunks.

One man, a big fellow whose black hair and beard hadn't seen a razor in weeks, stopped near the end of Adam's bunk. "Hey boys, look what we got here," he hollered. "We got us a farmer boy in the bunkhouse. We're gonna have fun tonight."

A tall, skinny man whose appearance was no better than the first came close, exhibiting a face that radiated pure malicious delight. "Yeah," he crowed, "gather round, boys. Sam has found us a shanty boy. There's a party in the men's place tonight."

"So tell us a story, shanty boy," the big man demanded. "All the new boys gotta tell us a story."

Adam opened his mouth but nothing came out. "Uh, I don't . . . know any stories," he finally managed.

"Then it's the horse blanket for you," said the tall thin man. He and another jack hurried outside.

"Well, farmer boy," Sam said with a grin that traced his cheeks from ear to ear. "Let's see how big a man you are." He swept Adam off his feet and carried him out the door, bracing his body like an armload of kindling. Effortlessly, he tossed the young man onto the blanket, which by this time lay spread on the ground near the shanty. In an instant, powerful fists grabbed the sides of the cover and flung Adam to the wind. Up in the air he went with arms and legs flailing like sticks in a tempest. Reaching his apex, he began to fall, dropping toward the spread at breakneck speed and expecting to hit with a thud; but he touched down as if on a feather bed and was tossed upward again, flipping and turning until at last he relaxed, and the ride went more smoothly.

Finally the jacks grew tired of the sport and opted for a new game. The cover was dropped onto the ground, and Adam staggered to his feet.

"Get the hat," someone shouted, and a scotch cap appeared out of nowhere.

"Now, young fella," Sam taunted, "this here's a little game we all play. You just put your face in the hat and someone'll touch your back—all you gotta do is tell us who did it. Then, if you're right, he goes in the hat."

It seemed reasonable enough to Adam, and he couldn't think of an escape anyway, so he dropped his face into the hat . . . and before you could say Jack Robinson, someone swatted his backside with a slap that would burn the hide off a ruddy rhinoceros.

Adam rose and looked around at a sea of faces, each with a grin that hollered, *Guilty!* With no likely culprit standing apart from the crowd, Adam pointed . . . and all the jacks convulsed with glee. "Nope, ya got it wrong," they shouted, so Adam returned to the hat with buns burning and a roar of hilarity punctuating the atmosphere.

Wham! Another swat, another guess, and no culprit.

Finally, after the third dip into the hat, Adam's rear burned like raw meat, and anger crept up his spine. He looked around at the men with blazing eyes and clenched fists. One more time in that hat, and he'd come up swinging.

But the clang of the triangle echoed on the air, and the woods men lost interest. They took off on the run toward the cook shanty, exposing a young jack squatted on the floor. Adam's temper flared, he cursed at the fellow and swung his fist, but the boy leapt out of reach and Adam missed the mark, which was probably a good thing. "I'm Harold Bosun," the young man said as they left the shanty.

"I guess we'll be swamping together tomorrow."

Great, Adam would be working with the lousy wretch who'd swatted the pants off him. He didn't know whether to pop Harold Bosun in the gut and walk away or just growl his resentment. He kept his composure, however, and accompanied the young man to the cook shanty.

"You gotta prove your worth," Harold said as they fell into step. "The guys like to have a little fun when a new boy comes around, but they don't mean no harm."

"Well, I hope they've had their fun," Adam responded. "Those men play a rough game of ball."

"Oh, they're not so bad. They just get a little bit rowdy, is all."

"You're tellin' me."

"Actually, it could be worse. Luc doesn't put up with too much stuff around here."

As the young men entered the building, Adam opened his mouth to speak, and Harold grabbed his arm, staring into his face and shaking his head. Adam looked around at the others in the room and noticed that all talk had ceased. He got the message and said no more.

Turning, Adam headed for a place at the table and was about to fling a leg over the bench when a big jack whose shoulders bulged like a bulldog shoved him out of the way. The big man took his place on the bench, glaring at Adam as though he were a sniveling cur. Then Adam tried for a second place at the table and was again pushed away. After about the third try, Adam looked up to see Harold sitting at the far end of the table with a c'mere grin on his face, so he made his way to Harold and found a place on the bench. Adam later learned that the bull cook ordered silence in the cook shanty and that seating was strictly ordered and adhered to.

The meal began, and the jacks filled their tin plates with beans and turnips and rutabagas, downing them with a single-mindedness that overpowered all else. Before long, a platter emptied and a jack called out, "More sowbelly down here." And the cookee brought a platter of fat salt pork. "Barkin' spider," called another jack—and the kitchen helper brought a fresh pot of beans. "Loggin' berries," a third man shouted, and the cookee brought stewed prunes. Within fifteen minutes the entire company had downed their meal, risen, and marched out the door, heading for another night in the close and smelly men's shanty.

But the day was not finished. Just as Adam arrived at the men's quarters, old Sam took center stage again. "Hey, farmer boy," he announced, "it's time for our bedtime story. Tell us a bedtime story." Adam's mind raced. He didn't need a repeat of the events that marked the afternoon. Although he didn't have a story to tell, he began to talk. "I once knew a young man named Seth," he said, "who ran away from his grandparents' farm without telling a soul where he was going."

Adam took a breath and went on. "'I know what I'll do,' Seth said to himself. 'I'll run away to the lumber camps where the sheriff can't find me.'" The new shanty boy noticed a collective spasm ripple across the room. Muscles twitched and brows furrowed. "Seth knew the sheriff wouldn't bother him in the woods," Adam said, "because lawmen don't like to mess with lumberjacks. They like to stay in town where it's safe."

A wave of laughter roared through the shanty as the men guffawed and slapped each other's backs and sides. Then Sam rose, took two giant strides toward the new boy and clapped him on the back with a whack that nearly knocked him off his feet. "It's nice to know you, Seth," he said. Cheers echoed through the men's shanty, as the men applauded themselves and commended their new partner.

"Oh no, I'm not . . ." But Adam let the matter pass. "Just call me Adam," he responded. He'd made the grade. The men had accepted him. He made his way to his bunk amid shouts of welcome and playful swats from the men. It had been a long day, and he was tired.

The young man slept soundly until early the next morning when he woke to a flurry of movement in the shanty. Several men rose, threw on heavy boots and coats, and headed for the exit. They opened the door and slipped out into the darkness. It was the teamsters' duty, he later learned, to rise early, feed and curry the horses, and be ready to haul sleighs when the other jacks finished breakfast. Adam lay back and returned to his dreaming.

But the reverie was not to last, for soon the door opened and a voice exploded into the morning. "Out of bed, you lazy varmints. What do you think you're doing, layin' around 'til all hours?" Adam looked around at his fellows to find them pushing back the blankets. Some men rose, dressed, and washed in the community basin; others threw on their cutoff pants, boots, and mackinaws and made their way outside into the icy morning, probably to relieve themselves. All awoke to face another day of intense labor.

Whatever their reaction to the dawn, the entire crew was up and about in time for the clang of the breakfast triangle. A horde of burly men left the shanty on the run.

In a matter of minutes they found their places at the table, consumed mountains of flapjacks, baked beans, and prunes, and then made their way outside where they dispersed into the woods. Adam followed Harold Bosun.

Soon the team arrived at the site where the two young men would spend the day. A jumble of fallen trees and branches and pine chips and sawdust littered the forest floor. What a mess!

"Well, this is it," Harold said. "Our job is to clean up this stuff so the horses can get in and haul the logs to the lake."

All morning Adam and Harold chopped away at the brush and debris. They cut branches and knots from a cluster of centuries old trees that had been laid to rest, and they cleared space so that the horses could haul the logs to the decking grounds by the lake.

After what seemed an eternity of chopping and hauling, lunchtime came, and the young men found seats on a nearby log. They filled their stomachs with baked-bean sandwiches and cold coffee. As they sat, Harold told Adam the story of the great forest and its harvest.

"When the crew reaches a site," he said, "the under-cutter surveys the work area. He plans the exact direction that a tree should fall and notches it to assure a landing exactly on target."

As his teammate spoke, Adam's imagination drew a picture in his mind. He could see the hewer swing the axe, burying it deep in the tree's bark. He observed as a notch began to appear in the giant's hide, widening with each blow. He followed the sawyers, as they moved in with their six-foot crosscut saw, and he stood nearby as they sprinkled turpentine on the tool to dissolve the sticky sap that oozed from the wounded giant.

"Usually they use a crosscut saw," Harold said. "They work together in rhythm until the tree falls."

Adam imagined he could see the men working. He watched the pull-pull motion that would lay the tree to rest. He observed the men as they hauled one way and then the other, biting deeper and deeper into the rings that marked over a hundred years of life. His imagination took the lead as the saw became pinched in the depths of the trunk and resisted the sawyer's attempts.

Turning, the lumbermen gathered steel wedges and pounded them into the opening that the saw had created. They jammed the wedges deep into the gap, leaving a wide slot for the saw's movement, cutting deeper and deeper into the tree's torso. At last a great *cr-a-ack* echoed through the air. "Timber-r-r!" the jacks called, and the death knell rang throughout the forest, announcing the passing of a titan.

Finally, Harold stuffed the last of his sandwich into his mouth and rose to his feet. "I guess we better get back to work," he said. The two young men made their way to the next fallen giant, stripping it of the last vestiges of life.

CHAPTER 25

HANNAH STOOD BEFORE her class at the little grade school in Hitchcock. She'd been teaching for three weeks now, ever since Verena Spencer married. "First, second, and third graders, you may go to the coatroom and get your things," she said. Faith Ann and Bobby Weaver rose from their desks, along with three other pupils, and headed toward the narrow passageway in the back of the room. Soon they returned, carrying snowsuits and boots, along with mittens and other winter apparel. "Okay, the rest of you may go," Hannah said, and the older students rose and went for their things.

Soon the classroom was filled with activity. Children were pulling on boots and snow pants and wrestling with scarves and mittens and hats and gloves. Some younger ones sat on the floor as they shoved their feet into leggings or hauled at cumbersome boots. Others, who were more adept at the task, leaned on desks or simply danced in midair as they wormed their way into their heavy winter gear. A few older students gave aid to younger ones, holding unwieldy garments and shoving boots onto little feet.

Finally, all the children were dressed and waiting for dismissal. Hannah walked to the back of the room, stood near the door, and called out. "Remember, sixth graders, your story about wild animals in winter is due Friday."

"Yes, Miss Hannah," the students responded.

Then Hannah dismissed the primary class. "First, second, and third graders, you may go." Three children grabbed their lunch pails and left the room, leaving Bobby Weaver and Faith Ann behind. "Grades four, five, and six, you're dismissed," Hannah said, and the older students exited as well.

"Okay," Hannah said, "you two bring in some firewood while I finish up in here."

Faith Ann and Bobby ran outside, returning shortly with arms full of split logs. They tossed their cache into the wood box and turned. "Okay, we're done," Faith Ann said. "Can we go out and play now?"

"I guess so." Hannah responded without looking up from the papers she was grading. "When I'm ready to go, I'll come outside and get you."

"I'll beat you to the swings," Bobby hollered, and he and Faith Ann ran out the door at full pace.

Hannah sighed and went about her business. She made lesson plans, swept the floor, and washed the board. She doused the fire and straightened her desk. Finally she slipped into her coat and went outside to find the children flying high in the swings. "C'mon, kids!" she called.

Faith Ann let her feet drag on the ground to slow her motion, but Bobby had another plan. "Watch me jump," he yelled. He let loose of the chain and soared through the air, tumbling headlong into the snow.

Hannah grinned. "Oh, you're a brave boy," she called, "but c'mon, we have to stop at Hitchcock's on the way home." The children ran to her side.

As they made their way along Birch Lake Road, the two youngsters ran ahead, stopping here and there to toss snowballs at one another or make snow angels or just to hassle the cold white fluff. At last they arrived at the store, and the children raced up the steps.

"Wait!" Hannah called. "Brush that snow off yourselves before you go inside." The children wiped and patted and stomped until Hannah came near. Then they all entered together.

"Well, how's our new schoolteacher?" Sam asked as they stepped inside. He reached into the candy jar and handed peppermint sticks to Faith Ann and Bobby.

"Okay, I guess," Hannah replied. She pulled off her mittens and scarf, smiling to see four loaves of Katherine's bread for sale on the counter. "I feel more comfortable in the classroom every day." She stuffed her gloves into her pocket and approached the counter. "The kids seem to respond well to me—at least at this point."

"Well, the town council was really pleased that you were able to take over after Verena and Buck tied the knot."

Hannah picked up a copy of the *Boyne City News* and laid it on the counter. "Thank you, Sam."

"Verena seemed pleased about it too," Sam, went on. "She said you'd make a good teacher."

Hannah's heart swelled. It pleased her to know that she was properly trained—at least as well-equipped as any who had preceded her. Someday, maybe, she'd attend that new teachers' academy down in Mt. Pleasant. It was said to be a special school where teachers were certified just like doctors and lawyers and other professional people. "Do you have any mail for us?" she asked.

Sam reached into the community box, drew out a packet of letters, and stood behind the counter, sorting leisurely through them. "There's one here from Clive," he said. "And there's one from your family in Ontario. Your grand-folks are pretty good about keeping in touch, aren't they?"

"Yes," Hannah responded. She winced, knowing all too well that the reason for their continued attention was Seth's disappearance . . . but at least now they knew that Seth had been in Hitchcock.

Sam turned his back to return her neighbors' mail to the community box.

"Thank you, Sam," Hannah said. "We'll see you later." She pulled open the door and stepped out into the cold, with Faith Ann and Bobby leading the way.

As they made their way along Birch Lake Road toward home, Hannah scanned the letters. There was one for Katherine from Clive and one for the family from Grandpa McLean, but none for her. She sighed and stuffed the letters into her briefcase—not that she cared about Adam, but at least he could let her know how he was doing with his search. She just hoped he was keeping his mind on the business of finding Seth.

Twenty minutes later, the group came near the Weavers' big old stone house. Bobby took off on the run, yelling his good-byes as he went. "G'bye Faith Ann," he hollered. "G'bye Miss Hannah." The boy turned in at the driveway and bounded up the steps and onto the porch. He flung open the back door and shouted. "Hey, Ma, I'm home." The door slammed behind him, and Hannah could imagine his coat tossed in a corner. She could almost hear Verna's voice, "Hang up your things and don't tramp water and mud all over the floor." Hannah and Faith Ann continued their trek toward home.

Soon they came near Camp 8, and the air was filled with the *yip-yip* of a mottled little puppy running down the lane. When Sassy came near, Faith Ann lifted the dog into her arms and was rewarded with a slobbery tongue all over her face. "No, Sassy, no kisses."

The girl put Sassy on the ground, and ran toward the cook shanty, leaving Hannah to make her way alone. As she walked, her thoughts returned to Adam. What was the meaning of that last night on the porch? Was he getting ideas just because she'd begun to get along with him? Well, he needn't let that moment in time define their relationship. She was a friend, and that was all. She set her jaw and started up the porch steps.

Later, as the afternoon passed into evening, Hannah sat grading papers while Katherine read the *Boyne City News.* "They got a new sheriff over in Boyne City," Katherine said. "And it looks like he's a pretty gutsy fellow."

Hannah penned a big B+ on the last paper and tucked it into her folder. "Why? What's he done?"

"Listen to this." Katherine pulled the lamp close and began to read. "New sheriff in Boyne City vows to arrest the lumberjack who's been tearing up the town. 'Big Jack Mackie will respect the law,' the sheriff said, 'or stay out of my town.'"

Hannah turned. "They say old Mackie got drunk and broke into some wealthy baron's estate. The guy is mad and threatening to run the whole police system out of town if something isn't done."

"It looks like this new sheriff's got a big fish on his plate," Katherine said. She folded the paper and laid it aside. "At any rate, we gotta get up early in the morning. I think I'll go to bed."

Hannah made her way behind the wall where Faith Ann lay sleeping. She crawled in beside the girl and curled around her for warmth. "Oh, Lord, take care of my brother and his friend," she whispered, "and remind them that I care." With that, she relaxed and fell asleep, not considering the fact that she'd just prayed to a God she didn't believe in.

Adam stood waiting outside the cook shanty when the door opened and Luc DuBois exited the building. With him came a big man with thick red hair and an unruly beard. "Adam Beste," Luc said, "Jimmy Denton went home yesterday, so I'm sending you to take his place. Fergus McMullin, here, will be your boss."

Fergus took an appraising glance at Adam and then he spoke. "Well, young man," he said, "get your things together, and I'll see you right here in the mornin'—and don't be late." The man turned, heading toward the blacksmith shop.

The next morning Adam stood waiting by the cook shanty door when Fergus McMullin came around a corner. With him came a boy about eighteen years old. "This is Dag Holm," Fergus said. "He'll be your partner. Now c'mon, let's go." The man turned and walked down the path toward the woods, with Adam and Dag close behind.

As they walked, Adam noticed the icy road, deliberately entrenched with ruts along its entire length. "The idea," Dag said, "is to control the loaded sleighs so they glide along the trench without slipping and sliding all over the place."

"It does look a little strange, though," Adam responded.

"The problem is," Dag went on, "the sleighs can run up on the horses and hurt or even kill them."

Just then a big sleigh full of logs burst over the hill, racing along the tracks with runners skimming the ruts. The driver stood atop, plying the reins and struggling to control the situation. Adam gulped as the bunk nearly swallowed the team.

"There," McMullin said. "You boys gotta keep that from happenin'. We don't need a team of horses gettin' killed by a runaway sleigh. Now get out there and get started." Almost before Fergus finished speaking, another team clattered over the hill with the driver atop the cargo.

"Okay, put the grit to her," McMullin called.

Dag and Adam shoveled sand into the ruts, and the sleigh slowed its pace. The animals tugged the load along with reasonable speed and control.

"Okay," McMullin said, "just keep 'em movin' and I'll check back later." The man walked away, heading for his own assignment. Throughout the day, the cargo kept breaking over the hilltop and throughout the day Adam and his friend shoveled sand into the ruts. The timber kept sliding along, making its way to the lake, until late in the afternoon. Then the bunks stopped coming. "Okay," Dag said, "Now we gotta clear the rollway."

Adam followed his friend along the ice road until they approached a bank that sloped downward toward the lake. He looked over the slope to find sludge and grit littering the ice. "We gotta clean that mess," Dag said.

The two young men scooped and shoveled and cleaned until the rollway was clear. Then they grabbed their shovels and headed toward camp. It had been a long day, and Adam was ready for supper.

CHAPTER 26

CLIVE SAT IN the DuBois camp office, reading the newspaper aloud. "New sheriff in Boyne City vows to arrest Big Jack Mackie." He looked up at Luc and Jasper who sat nearby and continued to read aloud. "That lumberjack will respect the law," the sheriff said, "or stay out of my town."

"Some difference between Sheriff Payne and that new Arpanyo guy they got," Jasper commented.

"Well, you gotta hand it to the guy," Luc interjected. "They say old Mackie's as tough as they come, and when he gets full of booze, he really tears things up."

"I guess Arpanyo's even talking about coming to the camps after him." Luc flicked a crumb off the table with his finger and shook his head. All three men knew the resulting disruption that such a maneuver would involve.

Suddenly the door flew open, and Fergus McMullin entered. He flung his turkey on the counter and looked at the boss. "I'm leavin'," he declared, "and I want my pay."

Luc leaned back in his chair and clasped his hands behind his head, smiling amiably at the hulk before him. "So, what's got your tail in a knot, Fergus?"

"Just tired of the place," Fergus responded. "There's too much interference and stupidity goin' on here."

"Listen, Fergus," Luc said, "why don't you just cool it for a while? Hang in here until you've had time to think. Then as soon as the season's over, you can go home with a full year's pay."

"Nope." McMullin's jaw was set in stone. "I'm leavin' this neck of the woods. I'm goin' home to Duluth."

"Okay," Luc responded. He hauled out the books and filled out the man's time sheet. Somewhere along the way, Fergus would find a local storekeeper who would be willing to trade cash for a Waterhouse note.

Fergus walked out the door, blustering at the world and haranguing at the camps.

Hannah sat at her desk in the schoolhouse fingering a letter she'd received the day before. It was written on a scrap of yellowed paper and enclosed in a ragged and dirty envelope. The stamp on the front looked old and shabby.

> *Dear Hannah,*
> *I'm okay. Don't worry*
> *Seth*

The young woman looked at the envelope. It was postmarked *Boyne City.* There was no return address and no indication as to how or where it might have been mailed. She laid the note aside and returned to her work, but the worn and sullied communication lay on the desk, inviting her attention and seducing her mind. She scanned the message again and sat contemplating her next move. Finally she put the student assignments aside, picked up her books, and headed home.

Later, when she entered the cook shanty at Camp 8, she found Katherine sitting on the couch, darning socks. "Look what came in the mail yesterday," she said.

Katherine wedged her needle over the darning egg in Faith Ann's stocking and reached out for the communication. "Well, it doesn't say much," she responded.

"That's true," Hannah said, "but I was thinking, we could send it to Adam and Clive and they could ride into town on the tote wagon and check it out."

"I doubt it'll do any good." Katherine responded. She set her mending aside and scanned the note. "But I guess it wouldn't do any harm."

That night Hannah wrote a letter to Adam.

Adam made his way to the camp store on a Sunday afternoon. "Any mail for me?" he said.

Storekeeper Marty Burch reached for a handful of letters the tote master had brought in the day before. He thumbed through the collection and pulled out a post. "Sure enough," he said. "Here's one from Hannah McLean."

A warm glow overspread Adam's body. It was strange what that girl could do to him. He tucked the letter into his pocket and made his way to the men's shanty. There he tore open the envelope, and a scrap of paper went spiraling onto the floor. He picked up the note and tossed it onto his bed, choosing to read Hannah's letter first.

Dear Adam,

How are you? Things are okay here, outside of the fact that we miss you and Clive. Faith Ann is as perky as always, and Cliffy just keeps getting bigger all the time.

I'm sending you a note that I received from Seth. As you can see, it's postmarked in Boyne City. Do you think it would be worth your time to go to town and check on it? Maybe you could talk to Clive and the two of you could go together.

Hope all is well with you. Waiting for your response.
Hannah

Adam's heart beat fast. He reached for the paper and unfolded it, scanning its message. Then his heart sank. There was almost nothing to go on and he doubted it would do a bit of good. Nevertheless, he'd talk to Clive at the earliest opportunity.

Seth stood with Wade Farley, watching as a great pine gave way and fell to the ground. It quaked and quivered, trembling on its boughs until its substance flowed out and it lay lifeless and unmoving. Then as the two young men moved in to remove the branches, a giant of a man came walking through the underbrush. "Here," the man said as Seth finished whacking off a big limb, "lemme help." The man reached down, grabbed the branch, and hurled it onto the brush heap.

"Thanks," Wade said. "You're really good at this stuff."

"Been doin' it for a long time," the man said. "I'm Fergus McMullin. I'm on my way to Duluth, and I need a place to sleep tonight. I'll give you an afternoon's work in return for a bed."

"Sounds good to me," Wade said. "But you'll have to talk to my pa about that." He pointed toward Max, who was some forty feet away notching the next tree. Fergus McMullin turned and walked toward the older man. Wade and Seth went back to work.

Soon Fergus returned. "The boss says it'll work," he said. He picked up a huge branch and flung it aside.

All afternoon the men chopped branches and moved logs and piled debris. Then later, when the team left the site, they'd finished a day and a half's work.

That evening Fergus McMullin stood near the cook shanty, talking with the men. He cracked his knuckles and spat into the snow. "They got a new sheriff over there in Boyne City," he said, "that's got a sweat bee in his overalls. He's gonna come out here to the camps and throw his weight around."

"Well, let 'im come," Max said. "We've got nothing to worry about, and he'll cause us no pain."

Without realizing it, Fergus had flung a dart into Seth's chest. Why would the sheriff come out in the woods? Maybe he was looking for a murderer. Whatever his reason, Seth would have to leave the Farleys—and he'd have to do it soon.

CHAPTER 27

ADAM REACHED INTO his pocket for Seth's note, holding it out to his friend. "Clive, I gotta talk to you," he said.

Clive took the memo, turned it over and said nothing.

"Well, what do you think?"

"It doesn't say much," Clive responded.

"No," Adam responded, "but it's recent. At least we know he's okay and he's out here somewhere."

Clive turned the paper, scanning the postmark and shaking his head. "It's a place to start, and that's about all. The truth is, Seth could be in the camps, or he could be on a farm—or he could be in a hole in the ground."

"Just the same, let's go into Boyne City and check it out."

Clive shrugged. "I suppose it couldn't hurt." He handed the note back to Adam. "I tell you what. I'll make arrangements for us to ride the tote wagon the next time it goes. We'll go to the post office and then stop at the sheriff's office. He likely won't have anything new, but as long as we're there, we might as well stop."

Five days later Adam and Clive climbed aboard the transport for their two-day trip to Boyne City.

With an aching heart, Seth reached for the pillowcase that had been his turkey and stuffed it with all his clothing, a comb and razor, and other supplies. He'd waited as long as he dared, and it was time for him to leave the Farley camp. "Here, I packed a few provisions for you," Harriet said as he entered the kitchen. "A good meal or two will help you on your way."

"Thank you, Harriet," Seth said. "You folks have been really good to me, and I'll never forget you." He pulled the rope on his turkey, closing the container of supplies and squeezing his relationship with this family from his heart. "But it's spring now, and my grand-folks will be looking for me. I have to be on my way," he lied.

The family exited the building and stood in the yard saying final farewells. "So long," Wade said. "It's been kinda nice having a brother to talk to."

Dean and Eric stood with tears running down their cheeks. "Goodbye, Uncle Jeb," they said.

Max slapped Seth on the back. "We'll miss you." Ike nodded his agreement.

"Goodby and good luck, Jeb Farley," Julie said. "It kinda feels like you're going off into nowhere."

Seth swallowed the lump in his throat. "It sorta does, doesn't it?" He turned and headed down the tote road. Seth was once again a runaway orphan. It was his life.

Two days later Seth slept on a bunk in the DuBois camp. The bed, he was told, belonged to a young farmer boy who had gone to Boyne City for the day.

The next morning, after a restless night's sleep, Seth shared breakfast in the cook shanty and headed north on foot toward the Farleys' old burned-out camp. As he walked, he thought of his time with the family. He thought of Eric and Dean playing in the puddle, soaked to the gills and happy as larks. He thought of the big wheels and the fire that had raged through the area, and he remembered the little bear cub that had shared his refuge under the bole of a tree. How had the little fellow managed without his mother? Had he found a surrogate, or was he making his way alone in a desolate world—a world of loneliness such as Seth himself knew?

At last the young man arrived at the deserted camp, and a rush of loneliness tugged at his heart. Mounds of black rubble lay everywhere, splattering the landscape with emptiness. He made his way to the river and walked along its bank, observing the icy flow and the swirls of debris that floated on its surface. It was a lonely place where life had once thrived and where now only desolation ruled. Looking closer, the young man spotted the raft that had ferried the Farleys across the water. He climbed aboard and poled his way to the other side.

Arriving on shore, he moved toward the deserted camp and built a fire in the old pit. He rustled through his turkey and found two biscuits and a chunk of dried pork. Then he took a seat on a log and consumed his supper.

As he ate, he looked up to see Roots hiding in the bushes. Tiny groans and squeals festered on the air as the little guy peered across the waterway. Then he turned and headed into the timberland.

Later, the young man moved into the Farleys' deserted shack and settled in for the night. Using his pack for a pillow, he fell asleep, dreaming of Ontario and home.

Clive and Adam hopped off the tote wagon in Boyne City and made their way along the boardwalk. "This could be a revealing day," Clive said, "or it could be a big flop."

"More likely a flop," Adam responded, "but we had to do it. Otherwise we would never know what might have been."

Before long, the two men entered the post office and took their place in line behind two women and a man. They waited while one woman bought stamps and the other mailed a package. Then the man picked up a certified letter and made his way out of the building.

Finally, Clive stepped forward and handed Seth's note to the teller. "Is there any way you can trace this?" he asked.

The man at the window examined the post, turning it this way and that. "I'm sorry," he said at last. "There's not a thing I can do for you." He returned the note to Clive. "It may have come from the camps, or it may have been dropped in the box right outside the building. Nobody knows. Actually, I can't believe it made its way through the system at all. It's a pretty poor piece of mail."

Clive shrugged. "Well, that's what we expected, but we thought we'd try."

With that Clive and Adam made their way across town to the sheriff's office and the probability of another defeat. "I hope he's a better man than Sheriff Payne," Adam said as they walked. "All I ever got from Payne was the brush-off."

"Well, you know, it really is nearly impossible to find someone in those woods."

"I realize that," Adam responded, "but somehow Sheriff Payne gave me the impression he didn't really care."

"Well, from what I hear, Arpanyo's a lot more dedicated to the job and a heap site more zealous than Payne was."

The two men walked along the boardwalk until they arrived at the police station. There they mounted the steps and entered the building, finally taking a seat in a well-lit office with finely polished wood floors.

A short plump man with graying hair looked across a desk at them. "Who shall I say is waiting, and what do you want?" he said. "Name's Clive Isaman," Clive responded. "I'm walker for the Waterhouse camps, and we have a missing person report."

Minutes later Clive and Adam sat across the desk from a middle-aged man with broad shoulders and a self-assured smile. "May I help you?" the man said. He nodded toward a couple of chairs, and Clive and Adam seated themselves.

"Sheriff Arpanyo," Clive said, "we've come to report a missing person. We know it's hard to find someone out here in this territory, but we don't want to leave any stone unturned."

The sheriff looked at his guests through his intense blue eyes. "Yes?"

Clive handed the note to the sheriff. "This came from my stepson a while ago," he said. "He's been missing for some time, and we want to be sure you know he's out there somewhere. We hope you'll keep an eye out for him."

The sheriff took the note, scanning it carefully. "Where was this fellow last seen?" he said, "and how long since this note arrived?" Adam told the story of Seth's disappearance, realizing the impossible nature of his request, but hoping against hope that the lawman would give the matter reasonable attention.

Arpanyo shook his head. "I don't know," he said. "A man can run off into those woods and never be seen again." He leaned forward, holding a pencil in his hand and tapping the eraser on the desk. "But I'll tell you what. I'm going into the camps soon. There's a jack out there that I want. Last time the fella came to town he broke into Baron Westchester's estate and created havoc for the entire area.

I'm going to get him or know the reason why." The sheriff handed Clive a couple of forms. "Fill out these papers, and I'll see what I can do. Don't expect too much, though. This guy could be hiding right under your nose and you'd never know it." The sheriff rose to his feet, signaling the end of the session.

Clive and Adam rose in sync, satisfied that they had done all they could to meet their objective. They stepped outside and headed for the coffee shop and supper.

The two men made their way to the café and then to the hotel, where they spent the night. The next morning they met Gabby at the depot and headed back to the camps.

CHAPTER 28

I T WAS A crisp spring morning, and Clive walked along the tote road toward Camp Rifkin with mixed emotions. Sheriff Arpanyo was coming to the woods, and he said he'd look for Seth while he was here. On the other hand, the affect it had on the camps was far from good. Ripples of discontent infected relationships, and fights broke out among the men at the mere mention of the lawman's arrival.

As Clive broke through the trees and into the clearing, he saw a wagon parked near the office. It was a classic model coach with skeleton-backed seats and a hardwood front panel. And there on the floor of the coach lay a chain and a pair of hand-cuffs. Arpanyo had arrived. The hardy woodsman entered the cook shanty to find the officer sitting at the table with two deputies. The men were fully armed and ready for any event. Burgess Walker, the camp caretaker, sat nearby.

"Well hello, Clive," Burgess called as he stepped inside. "C'mon in and take a load off your feet."

"Don't mind if I do," Clive responded. He hung his coat on the rack near the door and found a place at the table.

Burgess nodded in the direction of the lawmen. "I'd like you to meet our new sheriff," he said. "Name's Arpanyo and these are his deputies."

"Yes, we met some time ago while I was in town." Clive turned and smiled a greeting. "Hello, Sheriff, it's nice to see you again."

The sheriff nodded. "Hello Mr. . . . what did you say your name was?"

"Clive Isaman, I was in your office a week or so ago with a friend. We were looking for my stepson."

"Oh yes, Mr. Isaman, I remember you." The sheriff nodded in recognition. "You came in with that young fellow. I haven't forgotten your request. I'll keep an eye out for the young man."

Sheriff Arpanyo pulled a packet of papers from his breast pocket. His face grew increasingly dark and unyielding as he handed a photograph to Burgess. "This is the man I'm looking for," he said, "Big Jack Mackie."

Burgess took one look at the picture and his chin dropped onto the floor. "Fergus McMullin," he blurted.

"What?" The officer's face grew tense. "What did you say?"

"That's Fergus McMullin," Burgess said. "He's a good man—a bit rowdy sometimes—but a good worker."

The officer's face reddened, and the muscles in his jaw wrenched. "Well, he's not a good man when he comes to town; he's a drunken fool." The sheriff sunk his teeth into his roll with vengeance. "He broke into the Westchester estate and smashed everything in the place trying to get into the liquor cabinet. Baron Westchester's madder'n a crazed bull, and he's threatening mayhem with the entire sheriff's department."

Burgess passed the picture to Clive, and the man's eyes popped. Sure enough, it was Fergus McMullin, standing in the city square with a bottle in his hand, muscles flexed, and an arrogant grin on his face.

"Fergus left camp several days ago," Clive said. "I was there when he left. He said he was going to Duluth."

"Well, if that's where he is, he just better stay there, because if he ever shows up in my town again, I'll lock him up if it kills us both." Both deputies sat with glum faces, nodding their approval. "In the meantime," Sheriff Arpanyo said, "I'm gonna scour these camps 'til I know for sure he's gone.

Clive sighed and sipped his coffee. The area would remain in turmoil until the sheriff left the woods.

Adam lay on his bunk with eyes wide open, listening to the sounds of the night. Jeb Morse lay in his berth nearby, snoring like a turkey gobbler on rotgut. Harold Beal choked on his own tongue and rolled over with a gasp. Percy Williams tossed and turned on his pallet, causing the boards to creak and punctuating the air with the crackle of matted straw on wooden slats.

While many of the jacks resented Sheriff Arpanyo's intrusion into their lives, Adam secretly hailed his coming. He planned to remind Arpanyo that Seth was missing and that the sheriff had agreed to look for him. That way Adam could be sure the officer hadn't completely dismissed the problem, as Sheriff Payne had always done. Adam supposed it was just a matter of waiting and watching until the man arrived in camp.

As the young man lay contemplating his next move, one of the jacks rose, dressed, and pulled on his boots. The man reached for the turkey that lay at the foot of his bed, slung it over his shoulder, and moved toward the door. He exited the shanty without a backward glance.

Adam sighed and closed his eyes, trying to forget the incident. Then another man rose and followed the first—and another and another.

The next morning when the breakfast triangle rang, the company fell short of a full crew. The day would be difficult, but those who remained would pick up the slack, and the work would go on.

Seth shivered in the cold. He pulled his mackinaw close and headed toward Fort Mackinaw and an empty future. He leaned forward to face the drizzle that had besieged the entire day and drew his scotch cap down around his ears. He brushed the moisture out of his eyes and stumbled forward in the penetrating dampness.

In time the rain came to an end, but the icy cold continued to auger his bones, leaving him rigid and numb. Yet he staggered on.

Late in the afternoon, after walking all day, the young man grew hungry. He looked for a stump to sit on, but the entire world was soaking wet. He reached into his pack, retrieved a biscuit, and broke it in half, returning the remainder to its place for a later repast. He stuffed the food into his mouth and continued his trek, eating as he went. It was a toilsome journey over rough territory, but the man had no choice. He was an outlaw, and he dared not show his face in town. All afternoon he walked, ignoring the vertigo that haunted his body.

The young man's chest ached and his mind wavered. The earth reeled beneath his feet and his knees buckled, yet he plunged onward, wishing for a reprieve from the misery of it all, and he was rewarded. The world turned black and he knew no pain.

Hannah sat on her bed behind the dining room wall, reading and rereading Adam's latest communication.

Dear Hannah,

I received your letter with word that Seth is safe and somewhere in the area. I showed it to Clive and we went to the Boyne City post office, but they supplied no information at all. We filed a missing person report at the sheriff's office and were received well. Wow, that new Sheriff Arpanyo sure is a lot more helpful than Sheriff Payne ever was! It turned out he was planning a trip to the camps, looking for a man they call Big Jack Mackie, and he said he'd look for Seth while he was here.

I'm learning to handle most of the less complicated jobs in the camp and becoming more and more comfortable with the men, but I don't know that I want to be a lumberjack for the rest of my life. It's a hard and miserable job.

I haven't had a chance to go around the camps with Clive yet. I'm hoping it'll happen soon.

Missing you all. Somehow I've come to feel that Hitchcock is my home, and you folks are my family.

Hope all is well with you.

Adam

Hannah paused, remembering the touch of his lips that last night before he left. She shook her head at the stupidity of it all. Why would she allow herself to be canoodled like that? Did he think her feelings had changed that much? She stuffed the letter into the envelope and made her way to the kitchen to help Katherine prepare supper.

Seth opened his eyes to see nothing familiar in all the world. He lay on the floor of a cold damp hole in the ground. His lungs ached and his throat burned. A hiccup reverberated in his gullet and his stomach screamed its objection.

Turning his head, he saw a campfire flickering in the darkness and providing what little light and warmth was available. He was in a cave.

Then he heard it—the rustle of shrubbery shoved purposefully aside. A whisper of movement emanated on the air, and a man filled the entrance to the cavity, lean and sinewy with a tomahawk in his belt. Seth's body stiffened. He peered through the darkness, straining to see this intruder.

The Indian bent his shoulders and made his way into the cavern. He stood with head aslant, scanning the depths of the cavity. In the end he turned, staring straight at Seth.

Seth lay deathly still, straining against the pain in his body, afraid to make a sound.

At last, after what seemed an eternity, the stranger turned toward the fire and knelt on his haunches. He reached for a piece of wood and placed it in the flames, poking at the embers. The blaze kindled, and the cave brightened. Running Fox—the man was Tom Running Fox.

"Tom," Seth managed to say. "Tom Running Fox, is that you?" The Indian came near and looked down at Seth. His shadow trembled in the flickering flame. "Mr. Jeb, you awake," he said. "Me find you in woods. You lay on wet ground. That not good. Why you be here?"

Seth supplied the same lie he had been using for months. "I'm on my way . . . to my grandparents' . . . farm . . . in the Upper Peninsula," he said. "They've been looking for me ... all winter."

"You go too soon," Running Fox replied. "Now you sick. Be long time 'fore you go."

As the Indian spoke, the world tilted and went black again.

CHAPTER 29

SPRING HAD COME to the woods, and the snow was melting.

The river was overflowing its banks, and rollways were decked with a million feet of logs, ready for the river drive.

Sheriff Arpanyo had come and gone, having searched the woods and found no sign of his prey. Most of the jacks who had disappeared before Arpanyo's visit were filtering back, and life had almost returned to normal.

Yesterday the scaler had arrived, and he was hard at work measuring the harvest and branding the logs for easy recognition at the mill. The blacksmith shop was humming with life as Hans Bleeker rolled out extra pike poles and peavies for the event. Emma and her cookees were preparing meals for the river rats, and tomorrow the supplies would be loaded onto the wannigan for the trip downriver.

With the end of the season, some of the jacks would accompany the harvest, breaking up jams and herding the logs on their way. Others would head toward town and a world of bars and brothels. Local farmers, who had worked in the camps during the winter to augment their family's income, would follow the supply route home to wives and children. The camp would be deserted except for the summer watchman, who was expected in on the tote wagon at any time. The drive to the mill was about to begin.

Just now Adam found himself in the men's shanty, where the river hogs were preparing for their great adventure. Fred Mason sat on his bunk filing the calks on his boots to razor sharp points, while Dwayne Barber replaced the spikes in his Wellingtons. This calked footwear would help them to remain upright as they leapt from log to log, breaking up jams and keeping the drive moving.

The men gave little thought to earlier jacks who, over the years, had fallen into the rushing waters and been crushed to death by the stampede of logs. Although a good boss would try to locate the body and notify the family, many a jack had been crushed to pulp and unrecognizable. Often the unnamed body lay buried along the riverbank, never to be seen or heard of again.

The air in the men's shanty was blue with erotic talk as the jacks released a winter's worth of lust and deprivation. There was talk of saloons and rioting and women—and wild melees in the city. In his heart, Adam also looked forward to the end of the season. He missed Hitchcock and life at the Isamans' home . . . and Hannah.

Two days later, on April first, the year's harvest began its trip to market. It was four in the morning, and Dwayne Barber stood with Fred Mason on the skidway, ready to knock loose the wedges that held the logs at bay. The wannigan was loaded with chuck boxes and tools, waiting to accompany the trip down-stream, and the followup crew had readied their rafts for the task of retrieving strays.

These men would slog through icy waters, freeing logs that were caught in overhanging brush or sandbars and sending them on their way. They would be wet and miserable most of the time, and while they were safe from the crush of the logs, they might catch pneumonia and find themselves at the discretion of the camp cook for treatment.

Finally the moment came. "Break the skidways," Luc DuBois called. "Roll 'em out." Dwayne and Fred slammed the chocks aside, and a gigantic roar permeated the air as the logs hurtled into the water. The river drive had begun. The harvest was on its way to market.

It was five o'clock on a Saturday afternoon, and Hannah sat on her three-legged stool milking old Maudie. Squeeze and pull, squeeze and pull. With each tug on the teats, a stream of milk flowed into the pail between Hannah's knees. Then Maggie the cat came near, sitting with her mouth wide open, eyes half closed, and chin angled upward.

Hannah tilted her hand and aimed, squeezing the teat and sending a stream of milk between the cat's lips. Maggie hopped onto the bench and began to groom herself in normal feline fashion.

At that moment, the barn door swung open, sending Maggie skittering across the floor. "Hannah," Faith Ann yelled. "Are you about done? I'm hungry."

With the intrusion, Maudie grew restless and drew her hind foot forward, nearly kicking the bucket of milk out of kilter.

"Now Maudie," Hannah crooned, "just stand still and every-thing'll be okay." She leaned her head against the cow's side to reassure her that all was well and then continued the pull-squeeze motion that would provide sustenance for her family.

"I'll be done here in a little bit," Hannah responded. "I'm stripping the last teat right now."

"Okay, but Mama's ready, and I'm hungry."

Hannah gave a final squeeze and rose to her feet. She grabbed the bucket's handle with one hand and a leg of the stool with the other. She hung the stool on a nail and accompanied her sister to the cook shanty.

"Breakfast's ready," Katherine said as they entered. "You wash up, and I'll take care of the milk."

Hannah's stepmother reached for a two-quart jar that sat waiting on the cabinet. She placed a clean cloth over its lip and slowly poured milk through the fabric. When she finished, she folded the cloth with the filtered impurities and laid it aside.

Finally, the ladies found their places at the table, again acutely aware of the great gap marked by an empty chair. Hannah missed Clive, and she wondered how Adam was doing on his quest to find Seth.

Seth looked up into the most beautiful blue eyes he'd ever seen. He tried to sit up, but the room tilted, forcing him back onto the bed. "Who are you, and how did I get here?"

"I'm Mary Ann Hutchins," said the girl who sat at his side, "and this is my folks' cabin."

Mary Ann turned her attention across the room. "He's conscious, Ma," she called.

An older woman with wrinkled skin and yellow-gray hair came near. She brushed her hand over her apron and looked down at Seth. "Well, young man," she said, "you're back with us at last. We were beginning to think you meant to sleep the rest of your life away."

Seth reached toward the woman and every bone in his body groaned its objection. "Where am I?" he managed to intone.

"You're in the Hutchins' cabin," the woman responded. "Tom Running Fox brought you here some time ago."

"Tom Running Fox?" Seth paused. "How come? When did he . . . ? What was his . . . ?"

The woman bent and laid a hand on Seth's forehead. "Temperature's down," she said. "Tom found you in the woods, out cold and sicker'n a dog. So he brought you to us for help."

A wave of vertigo rippled over Seth's body and he fell back, breathing deeply to control the hurricane that thrashed in his stomach.

"You need some nourishment," the woman said. "Just a minute." She turned and walked away.

Mary Ann smiled and touched Seth's arm. "You've been in and out of consciousness for days," she said. "You were going on about some guy named Adam, and how you didn't mean it."

The young man groaned, wondering what he might have said and what this family might think of him. His heart wrenched, but his body was too tired to care.

Soon Mrs. Hutchins returned with a dish of broth and a spoon. She handed the container to Mary Ann. "See how much of this he can handle," she said. The older woman turned, leaving Mary Ann to care for her patient.

"Can you sit up?" Mary Ann said.

Seth pushed forward and the world reeled. "Ohhhhh," he slurred.

Mary Ann leaned close. She slipped her arm under his shoulder, and he could feel the warmth of her body. "Here," she murmured, "let's put these pillows behind your back so you can swallow more easily."

Seth lay against the cushions, content in the presence of this girl whose arms were soft and whose manner was so gentle.

Mary Ann spooned the soup into Seth's mouth and his stomach roiled. "Oooohhh," he groaned. He tried again and managed to swallow several sips of the nourishment before he heaved and almost tossed the soup into her lap. Then he fell back. "I'm sorry," he whispered. "My insides just won't take it." Mary Ann took the bowl and walked away. For several hours Seth lay immobile, drifting in and out of consciousness.

Finally, in the late afternoon the door opened, and a man entered. He threw his coat over a chair and hung his hat on a nail, exposing a bald head and a short, muscular body. He went to the counter, filled the washbasin with water, and began to freshen up. "We cut a good load of poles today," he said.

"Very good," Mrs. Hutchins responded. Then she opened a drawer, pulled out a clean towel, and handed it to the man. "By the way, our patient woke up this afternoon."

"Good . . . good." The head of the household wiped his hands and turned to look at Seth.

"He's resting right now, but he took a few sips of broth this afternoon. I think he'll be okay."

"Mr. Hutchins came near Seth's cot and stood looking down at him. "Well, young man," he said, "how're you doing?"

Seth looked up at his host with exhaustion saturating his body. "Hazel seems to think you'll be okay," the man said.

Seth smiled and nodded, breathing with slow calculated breaths. "You're looking a little green around the gills," Mr. Hutchins said. "But at least you're awake. That's one step up from yesterday."

He turned away, heading toward the other room. "Now you just lay there 'til you get your strength back."

Seth emitted a weak sigh, pondering the turn of events that found him nauseated and ailing, living in the house of strangers and dependent on them for sustenance.

CHAPTER 30

ADAM'S MIND AND heart were filled with mixed emotions as the tote wagon pounded its way along the rugged road on its way to the Rifkin camp. He'd collected his pay, his turkey lay at his feet with all his belongings in it, and he was going home—to Hitchcock and Hannah.

The problem was, he was going home without completing his mission. He hadn't found Seth. "Clive," he said at last, "it just seems wrong to go back without doing what I came here to do."

"Remember," Clive responded, "we're not giving up the search. We're just looking for Seth from a different location."

"But it still seems wrong to leave without doing what I came here to do." The young man grabbed the side of the wagon to avoid being flung to the winds by the heaving, jolting transport.

"Well think about this," Clive said. "Hannah actually saw and talked with Seth before he left Hitchcock, and she may have some information about his whereabouts that we haven't considered. When we get back, we'll talk to Hannah about the times they were together—things that were said. She may come up with some clue that will put us on track."

"I suppose," Adam responded. "But I still wish we'd found him while we were here."

"Yes, of course." Clive grabbed the wagon's side for balance and went on. "But you never know what may happen. When Faith Ann disappeared a few years ago, we thought the search was hopeless. Then Hannah remembered a single conversation she'd had with a friend—just a little comment—and it was entirely because of that interaction that we found the girl."

"You're right, of course," Adam said. "But that doesn't dispel the feeling of failure that plagues my mind and heart." At last, the wagon broke through the trees and entered the Rifkin camp. "C'mon," Clive said. "We'll check with Burgess to see if he's heard anything. Then we'll go for coffee." He rose, stretched his limbs, and climbed overboard.

Adam hopped easily onto the ground and headed for the camp office with his friend.

As they entered the building, Burgess came to greet them. "Well, Clive," he said, "how's it going?"

"Pretty much as usual," Clive responded. "The river drive has begun, and the camps are clearing out. About the only ones left are the summer watchmen and a few camp bosses. I'm ready to go home." Clive nudged Adam forward. "This is my friend, Adam Beste," he said. "He came to the camps with me last January. Do you remember?"

"Of course I remember." Burgess reached out a hand to Adam. "I see the bedbugs didn't eat too much of your hide, young man."

Adam flashed his best lumberjack grin. "I managed all right," he responded. "I just learned to slap those buggers in my sleep." A community chuckle resonated through the room.

"Burgess," Clive said, "I'm still looking for Seth McLean. We got a letter from home a while ago with a note enclosed. It was from Seth, and it was stamped in Boyne City, so we know he's out here somewhere."

"I'm sorry," Burgess replied. "I haven't heard a word. Apparently, the boy just doesn't want to be found. You can go home with a clear conscience." The man reached for his hat. "For now, let's go see if Molly has a fresh pot of coffee." They left the office, ambling easily toward the cook shanty.

"By the way," Burgess said as they walked, "what are you hearing about that new little boy you got this winter? What did you say his name is?"

"Name's Clifford," Clive responded. "We call him Cliffy, and he's the most beautiful baby ever born."

"I'm sure he is," Burgess said. The men entered the cook shanty to find Gabby Helms doing what Gabby always did, holding forth with some tall tale, regaling all who would listen.

"You remember," the man said, "I told you about old Fireproof Farley. He's the shanty boy who escaped that big fire with a bear for company? Well, now he's about done hisself in. That young sprog went and left the Farleys and ran off inta the woods alone." Gabby shook his head in apparent dismay. "And I hear he done come down with the collywobbles . . . fell down sicker'n a dog out there in the boondocks. He mighta laid right there 'til his whole body got et by the crows, if ole Tom Running Fox hadn't come along an' found 'im. He may be fireproof, but he ain't colic proof."

Adam and Clive took their places with the others, listening to Gabby's tale and grinning at the telling.

"I guess that ole Indian took the kid to some cabin out there in the woods an' left 'im. He was out colder'n death itself." Gabby flung his arms out, punctuating every word. "Who knows if he lived or died?"

At that point the storyteller leaned back and looked around the table at his audience. It was then that he noticed Adam. "About your age, he was. He kept talking in his sleep about Ontario—and he didn't mean it. An' he could never go back."

Adam's mind was afire. Seth! The young man was Seth, he was sure of it. The talk went on but Adam heard no more. He'd take the tote wagon back to the Farley camp, pick up what information he could and go from there. He wasn't going back to

Hannah without her brother after all. He would find that cabin or die trying.

That night Adam sat in the bunkhouse with his friend. "Clive," he said, "I can't go home with you."

Clive's brow shot upward. "Why, for Pete's sake?"

"You remember that story Gabby was telling, when we were in the cook shanty this afternoon? Well, the kid the Indian found in the woods was Seth. I'm sure of it."

Clive stroked his chin in contemplation. "What makes you think that?"

"Well, Gabby said he was my age, and he was talking about Ontario."

"And you're going to just wander around out here in the woods with no more to go on than that?"

"No, I'm going back to the Farleys and follow the trail from there."

"Then I'll go with you."

A spasm crossed Adam's face. "No, I don't think you should. I think you should go back home to the women. They need you, and if you don't show up, it'll scare 'em to death. This is something I can do . . . and you have a family to take care of."

Clive grimaced. "I suppose you're right, but remember I'll be worrying about you every minute and wondering what you're doing."

"I'll keep in touch. I promise."

The next day Clive headed out of the woods, leaving Adam to search for Seth alone.

Katherine sat in her rocker on the front porch, enjoying a moment of relaxation on a warm spring afternoon. Cliffy lay asleep in his cradle, and her domain was at peace. She lifted her eyes from the afghan she was knitting and looked across her family's cutover lumber camp. Clumps of snow still lay here and there on the cold moist earth, but the world had turned a corner, and spring was in the air. Her husband would be home soon, and life would return to normal. Together they would build this camp into a thriving farm.

Looking up Katherine saw, Faith Ann walking up the lane with her lunch pail in one hand and her reader in the other. Sassy, who lay sunning herself at Katherine's feet, leapt to attention and ran to meet the girl.

Faith Ann reached down to pet the dog, and it licked her face. Faith Ann sputtered, pulled away, and dried the spittle from her face with her sleeve. Then the two friends came walking side by side toward home.

As they neared the house, Faith Ann ran up the porch steps. "Mama, what's a stepdad?" she said. "Harold Flack says a stepdad is a second pa—like when you have one pa and you lose him, and then when you get another pa, he's a stepdad. Is Mr. Clive my stepdad?"

"Well, not exactly." Katherine brushed her hand over her hair and looked away, considering the best answer. How would she explain that Faith Ann's second dad was really her first dad, and her first dad was a stand in for her real dad? "Well, honey," she said, "a stepdad is someone who isn't your real pa but who takes care of you anyway."

"Yes, like Mr. Clive. He takes care of me, so he's my stepdad."

"Well, not exactly," Katherine said. "Mr. Clive is your real pa, but he wasn't around when you were born, and Frank McLean was, so he became your pa right after you were born, but Mr. Clive is your real pa."

Faith Ann stood with head tilted and brow furrowed. "So who's my stepdad?"

"Well just remember, your first dad was there when you were a baby, and he took good care of us. He loved you very much. And although we didn't want to lose him, we're okay now because we have Mr. Clive and Mr. Clive is your pa now."

Katherine felt her tongue getting twisted around her teeth, and she stopped short. "Hey," she said, "how would you like some cookies and milk? I have a fresh batch in the kitchen."

"Yeah," Faith Ann said. She took off on the run, and Katherine didn't even tell her to slow down. She was just glad to get out of that conversation.

"Mama," the little girl said as Katherine cut a slice of bread for a sandwich, "I miss Mr. Clive."

"Yes, sweetheart," Katherine responded, "we all miss Mr. Clive, and you can be sure he misses us. And he'll come home just as soon as he can."

Adam sat in the cook shanty at the Farley camp with Max and Ike Farley. "You're suggesting our Jeb isn't who he said he was?" Ike said.

"That's what I'm guessing. Seth McLean and I lived on the same street in Bounding, Ontario, and we were best friends. One day we went out crow hunting, and something happened. I don't know what it was, but I woke up in the doctor's office with a bullet hole through my shoulder. Seth was gone, and we never saw him again."

Wade's face grew contemplative. "I remember one day we when were out sitting on the codgers' bench, and Jeb told me he came from Ontario."

"Yes!" Adam nearly screamed in his excitement. "Your Jeb is my Seth; I'm sure of it. Do you have any idea where he went?"

"Not really," Max went on. "When he said he wanted to go to his grandpa's farm, we just assumed that was what he was doing. We helped him pack his things and sent him away with supplies to make the trip as easy as possible."

"What about any cabins in the area? Are you aware of any places where Tom Running Fox might have taken him?"

"Not really." Max rubbed his neck. "We just came in here this winter, you know."

Ike Farley lifted his cap and replaced it, adjusting it for comfort. "I suppose you could ask the watchman at DuBois. He's been here several summers now. And he has plenty of time on his hands with lots of chances to come to know people."

"Sounds good," Adam said. "I'll head over there tomorrow."

CHAPTER 31

A SENSE OF peace and serenity overspread Seth's soul as he and Doyle sat on the porch at the Hutchins' cabin. A world of huge towering trees hovered over the property on all sides, and a tiny lake rippled in the breeze not fifty yards away. "Mr. Hutchins," the young man said at last, "how long have you folks lived out here in the woods?"

"Well-l-l-l," Doyle Hutchins took a long draw on his pipe, "I'd say about sixteen years," he said. "We came here on an old wood-burning train when Boyne City was nothing more than a wide spot on the trail. There were two bars and a blacksmith shop, with a post office in the grocery store." Doyle blew a head of smoke into the air and went on with his talk. "There were no roads and no transportation, so I looked around and found a young farmer boy whose pa let him use the family wagon to haul our stuff out here."

Seth shook his head in wonderment. "It's hard to believe all the amazing things people faced when they settled this territory."

"Well, you do what you gotta do," Mr. Hutchins said. "We lugged our stuff down an old two-track path through the woods with mud holes and sand traps and creeks. Harriet rode part of the way with Mary Ann on her lap, but the two-track trace was so rough that it was easier to walk a lot of the time and carry the baby in her arms."

"So what did you do when you got here?" Seth asked.

"Actually the house was pretty much furnished," Doyle went on. "The people who had lived here just left everything and went back east, so we just shoved our things inside and took over. Harriet slept on the bed those first few nights with Mary Ann, and I slept on the floor 'til I could build a crib for the baby."

Seth leaned back, breathing in the fresh woodland air. What would it be like to grow old here in this remote place with Mary Ann and her folks? But the young man jerked himself back to reality. He must never allow himself to think such thoughts.

It was late in the afternoon when Adam entered the DuBois camp office to find Clause Buckler, the summer watchman, stringing leather laces through the eyes of his boots. "Well, come on in and have a seat," the man said.

Adam seated himself on one of the two chairs in the room and watched as Clause finished lacing his walkers and laid them aside. "Now then," the man said, "what do you want with me?"

"I'm looking for a friend," Adam said. "He's using the name Jeb Farley, and I guess he's staying at some cabin around here."

Clause's eyebrows lifted. "Oh, I've heard about Jeb Farley. They call him Fireproof Farley because he escaped that fire last winter under a fallen tree."

"Yes, that's him. I'm told Tom Running Fox found him in the woods a while ago, out cold and really sick. He took him to a cabin somewhere, and I'm trying to find him, wherever he is."

"Well, I can give you directions to a few of the cabins in the area. Got any idea where you want to start?"

Adam shrugged his shoulders. "Not really," he said. "What I'd like to do is stay here and use this as a base. I could sleep in the men's shanty and go to the various places as I have time."

"Sounds good to me," Clause said, "except you should stay here in the office. Then we could keep each other company."

"Great," Adam said. He tossed his turkey onto the extra bunk and reached out to shake hands with his host.

"Now then," Clause said, "let's go over to the cook shanty for supper." He pulled on his boots and moved toward the door.

As they approached the cook shanty, Clause said, "I suggest you start with the Rafferty cabin. It's only a few miles away, and you can make it in a day. You might be able to get back here for the night."

"All right then, that's the plan. I'll head out for the Raffertys' place in the morning."

Hannah sat at the table preparing tomorrow's lesson plans while Faith Ann played with Sassy on the floor nearby. Katherine sat in the rocking chair with Cliffy, singing softly with no apparent thought of the world around her.

It was then that the sound of footsteps resounded on the porch, and the most handsome man in all the world stepped through the door. "I'm home," he called.

Katherine flew to her feet with Cliffy in her arms. Hannah laid aside her books and rose to meet the man. But Faith Ann arrived first, clinging to Clive's side like glue. Clive swept the girl into his arms just as the others arrived, and the entire household fell into a community hug. The air reverberated with laughter and tears as Clive greeted each member of the family, squeezing shoulders and kissing cheeks and patting backs. Even Sassy joined in the excitement, slapping everyone in sight with her tail. There was noise and chatter and laughter.

Then Hannah noticed Adam's absence. "Hey, where's Adam?" she wanted to know. "Didn't he come back with you?"

Clive removed his coat and hung it by the door. "Actually, no," he said. "We were on our way out of the woods when old Gabby Helms dropped a clue about Seth's whereabouts, and there was no way Adam was coming home without first trying to follow up on it."

Hannah gulped. "Oh. What do you think are the chances that he'll find Seth?"

Clive shook his head. "I don't know. It doesn't look too good, but remember the chances weren't really good when you and Katherine went chasing after Faith Ann a few years ago."

Hannah stepped back. That was true. She supposed she'd just have to wait.

Adam had been at the DuBois camp for two weeks, he had visited several families in the area, and he was tired to the bone. Today he planned to visit a remote place over in Chippewa territory that Clause had recommended, and while he was glad for a new possibility, his soul cried out for relief. He was discouraged and disheartened, and each day brought another long hike into nowhere. The young man tossed his turkey over his shoulder and continued on his way.

Finally, late in the afternoon, he came upon an opening in the forest. There in the distance stood a well-kept clapboard house, a barn, and several outbuildings. He hurried across the field, anxious to find refuge.

As he came near, he met an older man walking toward the house with a pail of milk. "Halloooo," Adam called. "I was told the Bronson family lived near here. Might you be Tim Bronson?"

"That's right," the man responded. "And who might you be?"

"My name's Adam Beste," the young man responded. "I'm looking for a friend."

"Oh?" The man lifted his hat, rubbed his hand over his hair and then chucked the cap back into place. "And who might that be?"

"Name's Seth McLean, but I think he was using the name Jeb Farley."

Tim Bronson stepped back. His lips pinched into a thin line and his brow furrowed. "Jeb?" he said. "Jeb Farley?"

"Yes, I'm pretty sure that's the name he was using."

The man eyed Adam with a slow appraising stare. "Hasn't been anyone like that around here."

Adam's heart sank.

"So what's this young man done that you gotta chase him down?"

"I don't really know. We went hunting and I got hurt. When I woke up in the doctor's office, my friend was missing. We never saw him again."

Tim Bronson's eyes softened. He retrieved the milk and moved toward the house. "Well, come on in, young man," he said. "I'd like to hear about this fellow."

Soon Adam found himself retelling the story of Seth's disappearance and his own quest to rescue his friend from a lost world. As he spoke, the Bronsons seemed increasingly drawn into the telling.

At last Tim Bronson leaned back with his thumbs tucked under his suspenders. "Well-l-l," he drawled. "A young fellow who called himself Jeb Farley came by here a while ago. He stayed for a while and then left for his grandfolks' farm in the Upper Penninsula. Seemed like a really fine young man."

Adam shot upright in his chair. "That's him, I'm sure of it. How long ago?"

"It was last fall, Tim Bronson said. "Who knows where he might have gone from here?"

"How old was this young man?"

"Oh, I don't know, about your age."

"What did he look like?"

"Tall and lean with brown hair and a friendly face."

Adam's heart was filled with excitement. His blood pulsed through his system, urging him onward toward the goal. He'd found another link in the chain.

Several hours later Adam sat in the room his hosts had assigned him. Cautious excitement flowed in his veins. He took a pen and paper from a nearby desk and penned a letter.

Dear Hannah,

As you know by now, I'm still here in the woods looking for Seth. I've been running from one homestead to another with little or no success. Then today I met the Bronsons. Seth was here on their farm last fall. It's not much, but at least it brings me one step closer.

I'm spending the night here and will be on my way tomorrow. I guess that's all for now. Hope all is well with you and your folks. Tell them I said, "Hello."
I miss you,

Adam

The young man tucked the letter into an envelope and crawled into bed.

CHAPTER 32

I T WAS MID-APRIL, and Seth had been recovering in the Hutchins' cabin for several weeks. Just now, he sat in the sitting room listening to Mary Ann, as she played the old pump organ that had been brought in by horse and wagon some years ago. The music was beautiful, but then everything Mary Ann did was beautiful.

As the young woman pumped the pedals and the last strains of "Amazing Grace" trembled on the air, she turned. "Let's go out to the orchard and pick morels," she said. "There's a patch over on the east side of the hill."

"Sounds great," Seth responded. He reached for his jacket and slung it over his shoulders. "I need to be leaving for Ontario before long, and the exercise will do me good." He thought he saw a spasm cross Mary Ann's face, but it was quickly replaced with a smile. He pulled open the door and led the way outside into a warm spring morning.

As the two young folks walked across the land, the world blossomed with nature's transition from icy winter to early spring. Patches of leeks and spring beauty dotted the ground,

172

encouraged by the warming soil. They crested a knoll and looked down upon a secluded valley—and there, rising among the rotting stumps, were the mushrooms, dark and wrinkled and delicious-looking.

Mary Ann bent, picked several of the delicacies, and stuffed them into her carrier. "Pa'll be so pleased," she said. "Morels aren't available just any time, you know. They pop up in the spring and before you know it, they're gone." Seth bent to fill his basket. Then after the mushrooms were harvested, Mary Ann and Seth made their way across the fields toward the cabin.

As they walked, Mary Ann's hand brushed against Seth's wrist from time to time. Did she do that deliberately? His heart beat within him, but he mustn't let her know what he was feeling. In fact, he mustn't allow such ideas to cross his mind.

"Jeb," Mary Ann said, "do you ever think about settling down somewhere?"

"Not really," Seth lied. "My grandparents were expecting me last fall, and I'm already late."

Mary Ann leaned near and Seth's insides trembled. "What about you?" he said. "I suppose you'll marry one day and spend the rest of your life here in the woods?"

"Oh, I don't know," Mary Ann responded. "Maybe in time someone will come along and I'll be married, but for now there aren't a lot of possibilities. It's pretty remote out here, you know."

Seth's breath came in short gasps. He wanted to touch her, to feel her torso against his own, to taste the sweetness of her lips— but he stepped away; he dared not think such thoughts. He had to get away from this woman before he lost control and pulled her into an embrace.

Mary Ann looked up with troubled eyes. "Did I say something to hurt your feelings?"

The question ripped at Seth's soul. "Oh my goodness, no," he responded. "You didn't do anything. You've been perfect the whole time I was here."

Suddenly Mary Ann was in his arms. He didn't mean it but there she was. Their lips merged into a moment of perfect bliss. Seth's only thought was his desire to spend a lifetime with this girl. Moments later he released his hold. He stepped back with his heart throbbing. "Oh, Mary Ann," he whispered, "I should never have touched you. Please forgive me."

Mary Ann looked up. "Forgive you? There's nothing to forgive." Seth turned and walked onward with Mary Ann at his side.

His mind was in a whirl. He knew what he had to do. He couldn't allow his emotions to ruin that young girl's life.

That night, as darkness came and the world grew still, Seth crawled out of bed, slipped into his clothes, and stepped out into the night.

Clive sat on the couch with Cliffy in his arms while Katherine and the girls finished washing the supper dishes. He held the little boy to his chest and patted his back to calm his restlessness. He watched as Hannah stepped out the back door, flung the dishwater to the universe, and returned to the kitchen. Faith Ann wiped the last of the silverware, threw the dishtowel over the rack, and came dancing across the room to her father. She crawled onto the seat beside him.

"Mr. Clive," she said, "Harold says if Cliffy is my brother, you gotta be my daddy. Are you my daddy?"

Clive's breath caught in his throat. He wrapped his arm around his daughter's shoulders. "Yes, Faith Ann," he said, "I'm your daddy. You can count on it."

Faith Ann looked up into Clive's face and smiled. "Mr. Clive," she said, "I think you're the best daddy in the whole world."

It was several days after Seth had left the Hutchins' cabin, and he felt alone and heartsick. He hadn't even thought to bring his turkey, and he had no provisions. What a stupid thing to do. He had gathered a few eggs from a chicken coup yesterday, but that was about all he'd had to eat beyond some leeks and a few half-rotted potatoes he'd found in a basket near an old shed.

He wandered down a trail in the woods, not knowing where he was going but very much aware that he had to get away from the Hutchins family. If he stayed any longer, he'd give in to his heart's desire and ask Mary Ann to marry him.

Then the young man saw a glowing campfire just ahead. A man squatted nearby, poking at the flames. The aroma of roast rabbit floated on the air and the hunger in Seth's stomach rose in contentious demand. Maybe the man would share his meal. Seth made his way toward the enticement, watching and hoping.

As he came near, the man turned. It was Tom Running Fox. "Hello, Tom," Seth said.

The Indian raised his hand. "Hoya, *nenay* Jeb," he said. "You sit." Tom Running Fox pointed to a nearby log. "Why you be in woods 'gain?"

Seth seated himself on the log and began to weep. "Thank you for taking me to the Hutchins place," he mumbled.

"Is good you go, *nenay* Jeb, but why you be in woods again?" Seth sat with his shoulders slumped and his head sunk onto his chest. "I did the one thing I promised myself I'd never do," he said. "I fell in love with Mary Ann."

Tom Running Fox rose from his squatted position, came near, and sat beside Seth. "Tom think you hurt," he said. "Tom be sorry, but why that be bad?"

Seth felt himself collapsing onto the Indian's shoulder and pulled himself upright to regain control. "I'm a wanted man, and I don't dare to love anyone." A deep-seated moan escaped from the depths of his core.

The Indian laid a hand on Seth's shoulder. "Mr. Jeb," he said, "tell Tom Running Fox all 'bout it."

"I'm not Jeb," Seth went on. "I don't have a name. I've been lying for so long I hardly know who I am."

"Now you start from beginning. You need think what best to do."

Seth leaned forward with his elbows resting on his knees and his face buried in his hands. His thoughts wandered over the past, negotiating their way through an emotional wilderness. He felt dead inside. The air grew still, as he allowed the pent-up emotions that wracked his tortured mind and heart to flow outward. At last the words broke forth.

"Tom," he said. "My name is not Jeb. It's Seth, Seth McLean."

"Good meet you, Seth McLean," the Indian responded.

"I come from Canada, and the police are looking for me. I killed my best friend."

"Oh, bad," the Indian said. "How you get here?"

"I was out in the woods with my friend, and I shot him. He was dead. I don't remember anything. I just know he was dead . . . dead . . . dead." Seth's insides convulsed with pain.

"I ran. I ran and ran and ran. Finally I ended up on the beach in Michigan. I don't know how. I just know I'm a murderer. I shot my best friend. He was dead . . . dead."

Tom Running Fox touched Seth's knee. "Be okay," he said. "Be okay."

"Now here I am in the woods, and I don't dare to love anyone, not ever. I don't have a friend. I don't have a family, and I'm miserable. I've made a mess of my life."

"Tom Running Fox be sad. Good Book say you go back. It say tell 'bout sin and turn from bad way."

Seth clamped his eyes shut to withhold the tears that were forcing themselves forward. "I can't go back. They'll put me in jail, and I'll be there for the rest of my life."

"You go back," said the Indian. "God take care you. Give you peace. You see."

"I don't want to go to jail."

"You be okay, and heart be clean."

Finally Seth's emotions burst forth. He let loose of the fear that had gripped him for so long. "Oh, God," he cried, "I've sinned against you and against Adam and against myself."

With that confession, a shower of indescribable peace overspread Seth's soul. He raised his chin and squared his shoulders. "I have to go back," he said.

"That good," the Indian responded. "You face problem. God help you."

CHAPTER 33

SETH WAS FILLED with anxiety as he stood on the doorstep at Mary Ann's home. Should he just open the door and walk in? That's what he would have done a week ago. He doubled his hand into a wad and knocked. There was no answer, so he knocked again.

The door flew open, and Mary Ann filled the opening. "Jeb!" she cried. "Where were you? Why did you go off without letting us know? We've been worried sick." The girl threw her arms around Seth, holding him close as tears streamed from her eyes. Then she stepped back, apparently embarrassed by her outburst.

"Oh, hello, Tom Running Fox."

"How you be?" Tom said. "We come, talk 'bout life."

At that moment Mrs. Hutchins entered the room with a towel over her shoulder. "Mary Ann, what's all the ruck . . . ?" Tears filled her eyes as she hugged the young man and a patted him on the back.

A wave of acid surged in Seth's stomach. "I've been dishonest with you," he said. "Please don't hate me."

"Hate you?" Mary Ann said. "Jeb, I could never hate you."

"My name is not Jeb," Seth said. "My name is Seth, Seth McLean, and I've been lying to you all this time. Please sit down and listen to what I have to say."

Confusion and wonder clouded each woman's face as everyone present took a seat.

Then Seth poured out the story of his duplicity. It fell from his lips like acid from a broken vial. "I couldn't help it. I fell in love with you, Mary Ann. I tried not to, but it happened anyway."

Mary Ann's eyes filled with tears.

"I knew I couldn't make you my wife because I wasn't a free man. So I ran away."

"Oh Jeb—or Seth, or whatever your name is," Mary Ann's eyes brimmed with tears, "I don't know what to think . . . or do . . . or anything."

"All I can say," Seth mumbled, "is I'm sorry. Just don't hate me more than I hate myself."

At that point Mary Ann's mother spoke. "Whatever has been in the past," she said, "is gone. Now you need to look forward. You need to plan for the future."

Seth closed his eyes and wept silently, thanking God for these friends whom he'd only known for a few weeks."

"Why don't you stay here with us for now?" Hazel said. "There's plenty of time to take action when you've thought it through and you know what you're going to do."

Seth's heart broke. "The trouble is there'll be no future for me. I murdered a man, and I gotta pay for it."

"Nevertheless, take a day or two and get yourself together before you go back."

"Thank you, Hazel," Seth said. "I can never repay you for all you've done."

That afternoon Seth sat on the porch considering the direction he knew he had to take. He'd stay with the Hutchins family for a few days and then make his way back to Bounding and his error. Whatever happened, he would be at peace with himself.

It was early May as Adam made his way through the woodland. Apparently, April showers hadn't noticed the calendar change, for the skies were leaking a steady drizzle. He brushed his hand over his face to clear away the rainwater that dripped from his hair, his nose, and his eyebrows. It was not a good day to be wandering about in the wilderness. The young man wiped the rain from his face and walked on.

Noticing a tumbledown old shanty under the trees, he made his way toward it. No doubt, the cabin's owner had given up the fight for the land and left for better fields. Adam could sense the frustration of a trapper, or maybe a logger who had struggled to build a home here in the forest and then given up and gone his way, disillusioned and empty-handed.

Suddenly the young man's reverie was disrupted. The clouds opened, and a soaking rain came pouring down. He made a dash for the dilapidated old shanty, arriving on the doorstep cold and soaked. He pushed open the sagging door and entered into a shadowy world, fortified with a makeshift table, two handcrafted stools, and an old wooden pallet. He tossed his turkey on the bunk, pulled up a chair, and sat drumming his fingers on the homespun table. He'd have to wait out the downpour and then be on his way.

Suddenly the door flew open and a man burst inside, soaking wet and with water trickling down his neck. His face flushed red with exertion.

Adam bolted out of his chair, ready for any eventuality.

The man stopped, blinked, and stared at Adam in disbelief. "Who are you, and what are you doing here?"

"My name is Adam," the young man replied. "I just ducked into this place to get out of the rain."

The older man laughed. "Well, that makes two of us." He reached out his hand in invitation. "I'm Doyle Hutchins," he said. He pulled up a chair and took a seat. "I guess we might as well sit here and wait it out together."

"Well hello, Doyle Hutchins," Adam responded. He felt a little nonplussed at the mention of the man's name. "I'm on my way to your home."

Doyle's brow shot upward with surprise. "So, what do you hope to find at my place?" he said.

"I'm looking for a friend," Adam responded. Then he launched into an account of his travels and the reason for his mission. He spoke of his winter in the camps and of his visits with the Farleys and with Clause Buckler at the DuBoise Camp . . . and he told of the possibility that Seth had used the name Jeb Farley.

"Jeb Farley!" Doyle Hutchins shot upright in his chair. "Jeb Farley has been staying at our house for several weeks now. Tom Running Fox brought him in."

Instantly, adrenaline piqued in Adam's psyche. "Is he there now? Will he be there when you get home?"

Doyle shook his head. "No, I'm afraid not. He left in the middle of the night a couple days ago. We have no idea where he went or why."

As quickly as they had risen, Adam's spirits plummeted. He had missed his mark again. He looked out through the glassless window and noticed that the rain had let up.

"I guess we can go now," Doyle Hutchins said. "And we might as well go together, if you still want to visit my home."

"Sure," Adam responded. "Maybe you folks can give me an idea where I should go next."

Doyle moved toward the exit, and Adam followed.

Outside, in a freshly washed world, Adam noticed a new ambience. The sky was blue, the sun shone brightly, and a rainbow arched over the trees. Anticipation and discouragement wrestled in the young man's soul. He hadn't found his friend, and that was bad, but he was getting closer, and that was good.

Hannah sat on her bed behind the coatroom wall, reading and rereading the letter she held in her hand. "I miss those long talks we used to have, and I miss being with you and sharing our plans." The young woman's heart trembled with angst. Adam had become her friend and confidant, yet she felt unsure about him. He had been there with his support, yet she wanted to keep her distance.

She wanted him to like her, but she didn't want him to claim her. Turmoil filled her breast. Which way should she turn?

Adam and Doyle hadn't walked more than a half hour before a rolled-up cabin came into view. It was average size, with two windows in front and a roofed extension over the door. Smoke rose from its chimney, giving off the aroma of burning pine. "There it is," Doyle said. "You'll stay the night, won't you?"

"I'll stay the night," Adam responded, "but I want to get out early in the morning. I have a job to do."

The two men came near the cabin, and Doyle pushed open the back door. They entered to find Mrs. Hutchins standing at the range with her back turned. Doyle came near, put his arms around her waist, and gave her a quick squeeze. "Hazel," he said, "I found a replacement for Jeb."

The woman turned and looked at Adam with brows raised. "Well, hello, young man."

"It started pouring down rain," Doyle went on, "so I ran into that old shack on the Barker place, and there he was."

"Well, I have a surprise for you," Hazel responded. "We now have three guests in our home."

"Oh?" Doyle fell back in obvious surprise.

"Jeb came back this afternoon—and Tom Running Fox came with him."

A sudden spurt of adrenaline coursed through Adam's veins. His friend was on the other side of that wall, and he could see him momentarily.

"C'mon, I'll show you." Hazel moved toward the doorway, and Adam followed with his heart atremble.

He stepped through the opening and into the sitting room to find the object of his months-long search standing with his back turned.

A young woman about Hannah's age stood nearby.

"Seth," Adam called.

Seth turned, and his face glazed with shock. He stood as if wounded and waiting to fall. "Adam!" he yelped. "You're dead! What are you doing here? You're dead."

"No, Seth. I'm not dead. I'm okay."

"But you were dead. There was blood all over the place. You just laid there. You're dead."

"No, it was only a flesh wound. I wasn't dead. I was just in a state of shock."

Cognizance filled Seth's face and he fell onto the sofa with tears streaming from his eyes. "You're not dead. You're alive. And I'm not a murderer."

Then Adam spoke. "You saved my life," he said. "You took me to the doctor's office."

"I don't remember," Seth responded. "There was all that blood.

You were dead, and I ran."

"No, you didn't run; you saved my life. You took me to the doctor's office. When I woke up, Dr. Rogers was standing over me. The bullet went through my shoulder and never touched a thing."

"But you were dead. I shot you. You were dead." Seth sat weeping as the pain ebbed from his soul.

Adam sat by his friend, reassuring and comforting. Slowly, the Hutchins family melted from the room, leaving the young men alone to reclaim the past. Seth talked of recent days, running from the world, living in a chasm, and wishing for a new life. Adam talked of entering a lumber camp, questioning the jacks, and chasing from cabin to cabin. The lost was found, and a new life could begin.

It was evening of the same day, and Seth stood in the living room at the Hutchins home thinking about the future. He needed to return to Hitchcock and undo the harm he'd done. But now he was free. He was free to love Mary Ann. He had to talk to her, to discover if she cared for him as he cared for her. "Mary Ann," he said, "let's go for a walk."

"Sounds good," the young woman responded. She reached for a sweater, pulled it around her shoulders, and opened the door. The couple exited the cabin, walking along the path to the hill under a full moon.

Soon they stood by the lakeshore, listening to the water as it splashed among the reeds. "Mary Ann," Seth whispered, "do you think you could ever forgive me for lying to you?" He licked his lips, trying to swallow the lump that had deposited itself in his throat. Mary Ann leaned close and rested her head on his shoulder. "My dear Seth," she whispered, "I could never hold that against you. You were afraid and lonely. You did what you thought you had to do."

"But I lied to you. I knew it was wrong, and I lied to you."

"Shhhhh." Mary Ann looked up, touching her lips with her fingertips. "Don't even think such thoughts," she said. "We forgave you before we knew your pain."

Seth bent forward, allowing his lips to caress her forehead. Then she lifted her chin and their lips met . . . softly, deeply, longingly.

"Mary Ann," Seth whispered at last, "I have to go back to Hitchcock to make things right, but I wish with all my heart to make you my wife. Will you wait for me? I'll come back to you, I promise. Then we'll be together forever."

"I'll wait for you," Mary Ann whispered. She tilted her face to his and their lips met for one last time before they headed back toward the cabin.

CHAPTER 34

SCHOOL WAS OUT, and Hannah prepared to leave the building for summer. She finished checking files, computed final grades, and took care of her books. She swept the floor, washed the blackboard, and cleared the ashes from the little heater in the center of the room. Finally she closed the curtains and took her leave, reveling in the warm spring sunshine that covered the land.

Coming near the farm, she observed the open fields that Clive and Adam had cleared of stumps. There were several acres of new cropland just waiting to be sown with wheat or corn or maybe potatoes. She smiled at the thought of Adam's patience in the midst of her malice. He'd been far kinder to her than she deserved.

Soon Hannah mounted the porch steps at Camp 8. She pulled open the shanty door, and her heart leapt with joy. There at the table sat her brother, drinking coffee as though he'd been there all year long.

"Seth!" she cried.

Seth sprang to his feet and threw himself into her arms. "Hannah! I'm back and everything's okay." A sense of wholeness filled the atmosphere as the two siblings renewed contact and the family fell to visiting. The cook shanty at Camp 8 was filled with celebration until well into the night.

The next day Seth wrote a letter to his grandparents in Ontario.

Dear Grandma and Grandpa McLean,

I'm home! Adam found me in the woods and brought me back to Hitchcock. I thought I'd killed Adam and the police would come after me. Life has been lonely and difficult, but I made it, and now I'm free.

I met a young woman while I was gone. Her father is a jobber, cutting ties and posts for the L&M Railroad. We're planning to be married, so I'll be staying here in Michigan with her.

I love you very much. Please forgive me for the pain I've caused.

Seth

The young man carried the letter to Hitchcock's and posted it. The mail would soon be on its way to Ontario.

It had been several days since Adam and Seth had come home. An extra bunk had been set up in the tool shed, and both Seth and Adam were living in the building.

Adam, it seemed, was very much involved with everyone except Hannah, and she had come to realize that his only interest in her was because of his search for Seth—and that was good. She sighed, knowing she needn't worry about the man any longer.

Just now she sat on a log near Torrie's Spring, watching the water flow and wondering what the future might hold. "God," she whispered, "thank you for bringing Seth back to me. I can see now that you hold the world in your hands, and I want to be your child. If you have planned for me to become an old-maid schoolteacher, then that's what I'll be. I'll be the best teacher I can be."

Then a voice broke into the stillness. "It's nice out here in the woods." Hannah looked up to see Adam standing nearby. "It makes you feel close to God and nature."

The young woman nodded her agreement.

Without further comment Adam took a seat beside her on the log. "I missed you while I was gone," he said.

"We missed you guys too," Hannah responded, "but we got along okay."

Adam picked up a stick and started fiddling with it. "I thought about you a lot. It seemed almost as if we were close friends at one time."

"There were good times and there were bad times," Hannah responded. "Good times because we were planning to find Seth—and bad times when we were worrying about him."

"What do you know about Mary Ann?" Adam said.

"Not much, I guess she's a fine girl. Seth really likes her anyway."

"What do you think about his plans to marry her?"

"It's okay. I guess he's going back to her folks' place out in the woods, and her dad is going to roll up a cabin for them."

"What do you think about that?"

Hannah paused. "It would be better if he were here in town," she said, "but it could be worse too. He could go back to Ontario—or he could still be lost out there in the wasteland."

"Hannah, do you know that I love you?"

Hannah's heart did a flip. She hadn't counted on this.

Adam tossed the stick aside and stood. He reached out and pulled Hannah to her feet. "I've loved you since the day I first saw you."

Confusion rippled in Hannah's backbone. She'd been fighting this man's tenderness for months, trying not to care lest she should lose him as she'd lost every other person she held dear.

"I don't know," she responded. "Everything is so confused and uncertain."

The young man pulled her close, and her heart trembled. "I want to be with you for the rest of my life."

"But I thought ..."

Adam tilted her chin upward, and their lips met softly, gently, stirring a yearning that Hannah hadn't realized she harbored.

"Will you marry me?" he whispered.

Hannah's heart soared. She returned his embrace, setting her spirit free to care, allowing her heart the freedom to love. "Yes, Adam. I'll marry you."

Hannah would become Mrs. Adam Beste. She would no longer be that extra child who just hung around in a world that was not her own. She'd be an integral part of a real family, a family that cared and that was always there when help was needed.

Later, Hannah and Adam walked hand in hand toward Camp 8. She leaned in to her fiancé, dreaming of a beautiful future with this man who had been so kind to her since the day they met.

CHAPTER 35

I T WAS THE wedding of the year in the little town of Hitchcock. The church was decorated with roses, hydrangea, and chrysanthemums—all harvested from local gardens and precisely arranged by Aunt Mae. Neighbors, dressed in their Sunday best, were occupying the pews, and the air was filled with music. Molly Finch played the organ.

Katherine and Hazel Hutchins sat in the front pew as Parson Tibbs took his place on the platform. Next, Adam and Seth came from the prayer room, followed by the groomsmen and Bobby Weaver, who carried a pillow with rings tied to it.

The organ pealed, and the bridesmaids came down the center aisle, followed by Faith Ann, who strewed flower petals along the way. The ladies were resplendent in their beautiful new dresses, ordered from the Sears catalog. Mable Porter and Janice Mason took their places near the altar, and a moment of silence filled the air.

Suddenly the bridal march emanated across the sanctuary, impelling the congregation to its feet. Hannah and Mary Ann appeared at the entrance, resplendent in wedding gowns of satin that were planned and created by the town's best seamstress. Their hair had been carefully fashioned into upswept pompadours by Verena Williams, and their faces beamed with anticipation.

Slowly, Clive and Doyle escorted the young women down the aisle. "Who gives this woman?" Pastor Tibbs said. "Her mother and I," Clive responded. "Her mother and I," Doyle echoed. Then the men were seated beside Katherine and Hazel.

Katherine hardly heard the vows as she sat watching this girl who was her counterpart. She knew how it felt to lose your mother and father, to be left alone in the world with no blood relationship. At last Hannah would find completion. This marriage would give the girl a sense of belonging, just as it had done for Katherine when she had pledged herself to Frank McLean and later to Clive.

As the vows were completed, the bridal party turned to face the congregation.

"I present to you Mr. and Mrs. Adam Beste," the pastor said and then he turned, "and Mr. and Mrs. Seth McLean." In an instant the recessional filled the sanctuary. The bridal party walked down the aisle, waiting at the entrance to greet the congregation as they departed. They hugged and offered good wishes and shook hands.

When the greetings were finished, the newlyweds stepped outside into the sunshine of a beautiful September afternoon. Cheers filled the air. Handfuls of rice rained down on the happy couples as they ran across the yard and climbed into the community's first horseless carriage.

Clive cranked the engine into life and took his place on the driver's seat—and the just married couples rode away in resplendent glory toward a new life and a new world.

AFTERWORD

THAT NIGHT A party of young men slipped from their beds in the darkness. They trekked across town to the grange hall where they met in a secret confab. Jim Baylor carried an old cooking pot and a soup spoon, Marvin Short brought a cowbell, and Jack Ransom arrived with a dipper and a kettle. Everyone had a noisemaker.

Collectively they made their way to Camp 8.

Arriving at their destination, the young men moved swiftly toward the tool shed, where Hannah and Adam were to spend their first night together. Seven young men stood in the moonlight, ready for a grand extravaganza. Jim Baylor stood center-front with his soup spoon raised. He looked around at the group, paused, and brought the ladle down onto the cooking pot with a crash. The others activated their noisemakers in sync and the night was filled with commotion. There was yelling and laughter and clamor.

Soon Adam came to the door.

"Come on," Jim Baylor said. We're gonna go get Seth and Mary Ann. Hannah and Adam joined the group, and the community's rough riders made their way across the yard to the cook shanty where Seth and Mary Ann would spend the night—and the clatter was repeated.

Then the young men were invited inside and Katherine provided cookies and milk and coffee. There were goodies for everyone until late into the night.

When the young men left, and the shivaree was over, two young couples began their trek into a new world as lifelong partners.

www.ingramcontent.com/pod-product-compliance
Lightning Source LLC
Chambersburg PA
CBHW020844260626
47169CB00003B/1130